Life's a Pitch!

Life's a Pitch!

Andrew Akal

Copyright © 2024 Andrew Akal

The moral right of the author has been asserted.

Apart from any fair dealing for the purposes of research or private study, or criticism or review, as permitted under the Copyright, Designs and Patents Act 1988, this publication may only be reproduced, stored or transmitted, in any form or by any means, with the prior permission in writing of the publishers, or in the case of reprographic reproduction in accordance with the terms of licences issued by the Copyright Licensing Agency. Enquiries concerning reproduction outside those terms should be sent to the publishers.

This is a work of fiction. Names, characters, businesses, places, events and incidents are either the products of the author's imagination or used in a fictitious manner. Any resemblance to actual persons, living or dead, or actual events is purely coincidental.

Troubador Publishing Ltd
Unit E2 Airfield Business Park,
Harrison Road, Market Harborough,
Leicestershire. LE16 7UL
Tel: 0116 2792299
Email: books@troubador.co.uk
Web: www.troubador.co.uk

ISBN 978 1805144 533

British Library Cataloguing in Publication Data.
A catalogue record for this book is available from the British Library.

Printed and bound in Great Britain by 4edge Limited
Typeset in 11pt Minion Pro by Troubador Publishing Ltd, Leicester, UK

*This book is dedicated to my late Auntie Edna,
who inspired me to write and fulfil a dream…*

Author's Introduction

Now I'd like to start by saying you don't need to own a motorhome or a campervan or even a caravan to read and (hopefully enjoy) this book; it is not a pre-requisite or an unwritten rule. I know non-motorhomers and caravaners think we are a bit cliquey which has some truth, but it is a lifestyle anyone can embrace. As you will see as the story unfolds, we are all novices when it comes to living life in a tin box. Even when you have done it for a few years like me, you find yourself making a fool of yourself in front of your peers or saying something out of turn.

And whilst some who live the life might like to think so, it is not a cliquey club, or just for the over fifties. At the start of writing this book, we are still in the COVID pandemic and as a result, there has been a record amount of sales of motorhomes as people of all ages, sizes and backgrounds decide to take to the open road and get back to nature where, despite our great efforts to forget, is where we belong.

I decided to write this book partly because I love writing, partly because I am a motorhomer and partly because we all need a smile now and again. There is a slight possibility some of the events described in these pages have really happened in some shape or form before and you would be amazed which ones are in fact taken from real life experiences. However, any similarity to anyone living or dead is purely coincidental, or at least that's what my lawyer told me to say.

I may from time to time check in to add some of what I hope is useful extra info or advice – it will be in italics in brackets *[like this]* so feel free to ignore if I'm prattling on. If I don't hear from you, I'll assume things are all good and take that as a "yes" to start thinking about a sequel.

If at any point you feel the need to tear yourself away, do, especially for those necessary activities. However, there is always the option of having a nice shelf of books in your bathroom (as I have) which means you could read it from start to finish if someone is happy to bring you food and water.

Now I'll let you begin.

Chapter 1

Geoff Watt gazed at his dream motorhome, trying not to dribble down his Craghopper fleece that was just a tad too small for him these days. It was beyond his wildest dreams, he had made it, he now owned the latest and highest spec motorhome and here it was, parked on his drive for all to see.

He looked at himself in the sleek white bodywork like he was looking in a mirror. The chrome sparkled in the sunshine as he tentatively put his hand on the door handle and opened it with a smooth yet reassuring click. He stepped up into the cabin and gasped at the luxurious seating, the designer cupboards with built-in drinks cabinet and the huge flatscreen TV with gadgets galore.

His neighbour Colin had told him you can 'sync' everything to your phone these days, so he opened the app he had downloaded in a frenzy when the delivery man had arrived and started to press every picture of electronic appliances on the screen.

What was going on? Nothing was happening! All he could hear was his phone buzzing constantly at him, as if telling him he and technology were just not a match made in heaven.

Janice always said "Geoff, you and that bloody phone, it's like having another child at home, it never does as you ask it to!"

The buzzing got louder and louder and Geoff felt a strange sensation in his wrist. Oh no, is this the start of some terrible illness? They say it always starts with tremors! What if it gets worse? They won't let him drive his dream camper, he won't be able to do all those things he and Janice have been planning for years, he won't be able to live the dream!

Geoff opened his eyes. The Fitbit on his wrist continued to buzz. He looked at it and his bleary eyes tried to focus on the time. 08.01am came blurrily into view and reality slowly started to dawn on him.

"Turn that bloody thing off!" Janice said as she rolled over and elbowed him in the ribs. "I don't know why you wear that thing. It doesn't work properly and your days of being a "fit bit" are well and truly over!"

Geoff sighed. Janice was convinced his Fitbit counted more steps than hers and somehow he was cheating in the fitness battle they had started when they got them for each other last Christmas.

He pressed the button and the buzzing stopped and with it his memories of his dream motorhome. But today was going to get better. Today was the day. Today was the National Motorhome Exhibition and it was being held in their home town in Beddlesford, West Yorkshire for the very first time. Geoff had got his tickets online, a whopping saving of 10% although Janice said £1.50 off each ticket was not going to light up the world! Funny that, 10% off the clothes she buys was always sold to Geoff as a game changer, a once in a lifetime bargain that he would be daft to turn his nose up at. And here he was, doing his bit for the "motorhome" fund that would continue their way out of the rat race they had fallen into like so many others.

At 55, Geoff had done ok for himself in his career. He had spent 30 years working his way up the ranks of the corporate world and had eventually been getting paid very well solving everyone else's problems. And now he was free, taking advantage of a timely redundancy offer and a nice pension lump sum to pay off the rest of their mortgage and live a little.

Geoff's background in financial services meant he had made sure there was enough left to give them a good income when they needed it most but he knew he would need to find something to do at some point to keep his brain ticking and maintain the comfortable lifestyle they had made for themselves. In the meantime, this new found freedom and the prospect of owning their own motorhome was going to be like a new lease of life.

Janice was just that little bit younger than Geoff and she never missed an opportunity to remind him. Her 50th was coming up soon and for a few months at least, Geoff could wheel out the "do you think you should be doing that at your age?" line without Janice's usual "Well I'll never be as old as you" retort. Janice ran her own business from home as an artist, painting landscapes mainly but sometimes pencil drawings too and she was very good at it.

She was self-taught and had set up her art business around 10 years ago after a friend said one of her paintings was good enough to buy and then went and offered her £50 for it! After much encouraging by Geoff, Janice got a website set up and away she went. She always underplayed how good she was and how important her business was in helping them both enjoy life but deep down it made her feel good when Geoff reminded her she was a creative genius!

Janice took a little longer than Geoff to warm to the prospect of buying a motorhome, but her years spent as a young girl on caravan holidays in Primrose Valley had etched something in her heart and the thought of returning to those carefree days and the prospect of painting in the outdoors was enough to bring her round to the idea and now she realised it was something she and Geoff could share together as they grew older. Despite the bravado, Janice loves Geoff deeply, as he does her. They took a bit of time to find each other but when they did, they knew. Isn't it nice when that happens?

Geoff leaned over to Janice. "Morning gorgeous, I love you."

"Morning darling, I love you too!" replied Janice and with that, they completed their morning ritual of exchanging three quick kisses on the lips. They'd started doing this when they began courting *[that's dating to the under 40s]* and had never missed a day, except when Geoff was away down in London with work. They both agreed if you can't take a few seconds to say it, then it's not much good is it? Got a point I think.

Geoff smiled and got out of bed. He made his usual trip to the bathroom for his morning wee. He was in pretty good health but a year ago he was finding himself getting up for a wee a few times a night and it turned out his prostate had decided to go on a growing spurt at the wrong time of life! A rather painful procedure and a scan later and he was relieved to hear it was nothing a daily tablet wouldn't keep under control.

Chapter 2

Geoff made his way downstairs to feed Mabel. Mabel was a rather chunky cocker spaniel, white except for a few brown splashes, including across one eye which made her just about the cutest dog you could ever see. And didn't she know it! Geoff recalled how Janice and their daughter Gail had set up an account on the internet when she was a puppy, one of those "Instaface" accounts Geoff called it, and she now had more followers than her from The One Show, Alex Johnson? Jones? Whatever!

He opened the kitchen door and there she was, sat in her basket, the tip of her tail wagging like a rattlesnake and her big "butter wouldn't melt" eyes telling him she was ready for her breakfast.

"Not until you've had a wee," Geoff said as he gave her his usual pat on the head and then a tickle of her tummy as she put her front legs on his belly and stretched out in anticipation. That tummy tickle first thing was just the ticket and Mabel then ran down the garden for her obligatory wee while Geoff got her breakfast ready.

Mabel knew she needed to complete the routine or she'd be sent back down the garden so she always glanced back at Geoff to see if he was watching. Sometimes she'd do a little stoop knowing he couldn't see if she was really having a wee, and then sprint back into the house very proud of herself. Today however, she was bursting for a wee as she'd drank a lot of water from her bowl before heading off to bed last night.

"Mabel!" Geoff shouted. Still the wee flowed. "Mabel!!" Geoff shouted even louder.

"Not quite done yet," Mabel thought. "Just one more squeeze and "Ahhhh, that's it, all done!"

Mission accomplished she ran back into the kitchen just in time to see Geoff serving up her yummy breakfast of raw duck and chicken. Geoff felt a bit queasy as he chopped up the meat and poured a bit of the excess blood into her dish.

"Urrrgh Mabel, I don't know how you eat this stuff!!" He said as he put the dish down on the floor and Mabel sat down waiting for the signal.

"Wait, ready, steady, go!" Geoff said and Mabel dived into the bowl headfirst with all the finesse of a raging lion mauling his prey.

"I don't know," Geoff said "if all those Instaface followers could see you now! They wouldn't be messaging all those soppy messages then!"

As Mabel wolfed down her meal, Geoff glanced at the calendar on the wall at today's date. Saturday 20th May had the words "Motorhome Show" with three exclamations after it. And here he was, only a couple of hours away from wandering amongst the finest collection of motorhomes in the country.

"Morning," came the subdued words from Gail as she walked into the kitchen, still half asleep. Gail was 16 years old and the only child of Geoff and Janice. They had wanted more, but they met later in life than they would have liked, both after previous marriages, and time had caught up with them.

Gail was a good kid, no trouble really, but now in her first year of doing her A Levels, she was feeling the strain and not too happy about being roused from her weekend sleep by dad shouting "Mabel" at the top of his voice right underneath her bedroom window.

"Morning," Geoff replied. "What are you doing up so early on a Saturday? Not like you, don't normally see you before 11. Usually you are…"

"You woke me up shouting Mabel!" growled Gail. "And probably half the street!" Gail sat down at the breakfast bar and flopped forward as if she had no bones in her upper body. "Now I'll never get back to sleep!"

"Well, how can you sleep on the most exciting day of the year!" Geoff said pointing at the calendar and then proceeded to do some sort of dad dance around the kitchen floor, something he'd seen in a Steve Martin film once, although Geoff thought his moves were much cooler.

"Dad, what ARE you doing?" said Gail. "Do you know who you look like? Katie's grandad when we went to his 80th birthday do last year. You know, the one when he tripped over dancing to the Bee Gees and it all had to end early when the ambulance came."

"Naaaah," said Geoff. "He was a right old codger. Your dad has got moves man, rhythm man."

"Why are you talking like a Jamaican man dad? Mum

sat down at that party when you started dancing like that. She said you were embarrassing her. In fact, everyone sat down!"

"Course they did love. They wanted to watch a master at work!" He continued to shuffle left and right and decided to finish with his legendary spin. Next thing he knew, Geoff was on the floor with Mabel licking his face. Unfortunately, he'd forgotten to close his mouth and Mabel managed to slip her extra long tongue between his lips. To his horror, Geoff felt the menacing tongue touch his top front teeth and then became aware of a strange metal taste.

"Urrrgh gerroff Mabel!! She's tongued me, she's only bloody tongued me! Its raw duck and chicken!! Urrrgh, Gail get me some orange juice from the fridge, quick!"

Gail ran for a glass and poured some juice into it and handed it to Geoff who had now slumped up against the dishwasher door. Geoff gulped the orange down, desperately trying not think about how long that duck or chicken had been dead.

"Told you dad. Mum'll have a fit when she comes down."

"Fit about what?" said Janice as she came into the kitchen. "What was all that noise about? Geoff, have you been shouting at Mabel again? What are you doing on the floor you daft lump?"

Mabel ran up to Janice, tail wagging round and round like a propellor, her big eyes just that little bit wider than when Geoff greeted her.

"Awww, where's my little girl! What's daddy been shouting at you for? The nasty man, don't listen to him.

Have you had your breakfast?" She said it twice, as if giving Mabel more time to reply.

"Oh yes you have, I can see a bit of duck gristle on the side of your little mouth. Geoff – have you not wiped her mouth? You know she ends up rubbing it on the sofa and the living room ends up smelling like an abattoir. I don't know, do I have to do everything myself? And get up off the floor man. What is your father doing?"

"Beats me mum. One minute he thinks he's Justin Timberlake, the next he's trying to french kiss Mabel. I think he's having a bit of a midlife crisis."

Geoff looked at them both and sighed. This was his day and he was going to enjoy it. "Take a deep breath and then take another," he thought, tentatively running his own tongue round his mouth and relieved to taste orange, albeit it had a tinge of duck l'orange.

"In less than two hours I'll be in heaven," he said.

"You bloody will be if you keep thinking you're twenty-five again, you silly man. Come on, it's your turn to make breakfast."

Gail, now wide awake, got off the breakfast bar stool she'd been perched on and grabbed her phone from the sideboard. Although 16 years old, she knew she wasn't allowed her phone in her room overnight, so she remembered she'd forgotten her first golden rule which was to check her messages. She scrolled and pressed and scrolled and pressed. Her eyes squinted and then widened. She dropped her phone with a clatter on the side board and proceeded to wave her arms about and dance a little jig like a cross between Magnus Pike and Michael Flatley, not that she would know who either of them were.

"Chelsea and Chesney have split up!" she said repeatedly in a sort of voice Geoff had heard by a rapper when he was flicking through the music channels on the TV. Gail's rapping and mad Riverdance continued with no change in lyrics until she suddenly froze.

"So that means he's free for me!" she cried and with that she grabbed her phone and resumed her performance all the way out of the kitchen and back up the stairs. Five seconds later, Geoff heard her bedroom door close and knew Gail would be texting her friends to plot her plan to capture Chesney. "Chesney?" Geoff said. "Who calls their kid Chesney these days?" Geoff said to Janice.

"Well they don't do they? I know his mum Aretha and she told me they named him after Chesney Hawkes after that song, you know, The One and Only."

"I bet he is the bloody one and only," said Geoff with a chuckle. "Chesney bloody Hawkes!"

"Anyway," he thought "Soon we'll be motoring. Let the adventure begin Janice!"

Chapter 3

Geoff opened the front door and stepped out into the driveway at No 6 Sycamore Avenue. He surveyed the dark grey with white speckles resin driveway that had been laid three months ago in preparation for their new arrival. "That'll take a ten tonne truck that drive will," the foreman of the company had said as Geoff carried out his inspection the day after it had dried out nicely. "So don't worry about a 3 tonne campervan," he carried on.

"It's not a campervan!" Geoff snapped and then smiled "It's a motorhome, streamlined, coach built and as luxurious as a Premier Inn inside!" he added.

"Oh," said the foreman "all purple inside is it?"

"What a heathen," Geoff thought as he unlocked the car. "Doesn't know the difference between a camper and a motorhome! Some people…"

"Alright Geoff," came a loud shout from across the road. Geoff looked up and saw Colin Jackson *[no not that one!]* his neighbour and good friend waving at him frantically.

"Today's the big day then? Bet you can't wait to get

there and find your camperv…I I mmmean luxury motorhome," Colin stuttered.

Geoff and Colin had lived opposite each other for around 5 years, Geoff at No 6 and Colin at No 7. They had become friends after they both reversed their cars off their drives and into each other two days after Geoff and Janice had moved in. Milliseconds after the crunch of bumpers, Geoff and Colin jumped out of their cars and ran to see the damage.

"Look what you've done!" said Geoff.

"Look what *you've* done!" said Colin.

"Whadduya mean?" said Geoff. "I was halfway out of my drive when you came racing out like Lewis bloody Hamilton!"

"Rubbish!" said Colin. "I looked in my mirror and you were still sat in your drive and your reverse lights weren't even on! And anyway, Lewis Hamilton doesn't drive backwards!"

"Yeh, and he doesn't drive one of them either!" Geoff said, feeling he was getting the upper hand.

"And what's wrong with a Skoda?" asked Colin. "Best mpg in its class!"

"Yeh, and the only one in its class!" continued Geoff. Now feeling like he was making his mark.

"Well yours is an old man's car!" replied Colin, realising he needed a good recovery to save face. Other neighbours curtains were starting to twitch and he wasn't going to be shown up by a new kid on the block, well old kid really.

"My dad got one of those when he retired. Said it was for the more *mature* and *sophisticated* driver…and by that he meant *old*."

"I'll give you old…!" shouted Geoff, just as Janice grabbed his arm and glared at him furiously.

"What the heck do you think you're doing man? We've been here two minutes and you're fighting with the neighbours." She'd heard the crash of plastic and metal and come out to see what all the commotion was.

At the same time, Pat emerged from Colin's front door and ran to Colin's side. "What's happened?" she said to Colin. "Have you been hurt? Here, look into my eyes, look at my fingers, how many are there? Are you concussed? Have you got whiplash?"

"Stop fretting woman. I was just getting whatsisname here to own up to this mess!"

"It's Geoff and it was your fault. And ay, Janice, how about seeing if I'm seriously injured? I may have long lasting injuries and PDST!" And who's got CCTV around here?" Geoff started to look around at the neighbours houses for evidence while the curtains shuffled in all the front windows, up and downstairs.

"It's PTSD you idiot and the only one here with that is me after 18 years living with you! Look you two, I'm Janice and I'm sure we can sort this out. Maybe over dinner? We'd love to invite you over, wouldn't we Geoff?"

Geoff sighed. He couldn't see any CCTV and doubted whether any of the curtain twitchers would be on his side.

"Well, as long as they bring a decent bottle of red. None of that three for a tenner stuff!"

Janice walked up to Pat. "I'm Janice, pleased to meet you. Sorry about Geoff. I say that a lot."

"I'm Pat," said Pat. "And don't worry, Colin's the same.

I have a feeling we are going to have our work cut out with these two!"

They settled on a 50/50 split of the damages over dinner and a nice bottle of Rioja and Geoff and Colin reluctantly shook hands. By the end of the evening the whole episode was forgotten and they realised they may just have more in common than being neighbours in Sycamore Avenue. They both loved live music and the outdoors which generated lots of laughter and they also were living life in the rat race, which brought moans and groans.

"I'm not going to wait until I'm too old to enjoy life before I get out!" concluded Geoff and everyone clinked their glasses and drank to that!

When Geoff and Janice eventually waved their neighbours goodbye and closed the front door, Janice turned to Geoff and said "It's going to be lovely living here. Don't mess it up!!"

Colin and Pat were a little younger than Geoff and Janice and had a son called Robbie, who was just a few months younger than Gail. Colin worked in the town at a branch for a big high street bank, while Pat was a primary school teacher. The four of them began their friendship with that dinner and had never looked back. Over the next five years things blossomed and they grew to be close friends, often being there for each other when the occasion called.

Still, it had continued to be a bone of contention who was at fault in the original 'clash of the titans' as the boys called it, with Colin claiming he had moved off first and Geoff claiming Colin couldn't make the first move if he tried. When they saw the playground squabble becoming in danger of a schoolboy scrap, either Janice or Pat would intervene and remind them of their age.

Geoff walked to the end of his drive. "Yep, setting off when Janice has finished putting her face on," Geoff said. "Just checking I've got all my info in the back seat. Why don't you come with us? It'll be great, just imagine the four of us exploring the undiscovered corners of the globe." Geoff's eyes gazed around the landscape of Sycamore Drive as if he was surveying unchartered waters.

"No thanks," said Colin. Pat's got a list of jobs as long as my arm and anyway, camping on wheels isn't for me, give me a Premier Inn any day!"

Geoff had been trying to persuade Colin to get into the mood for motorhome living without success. Colin liked his creature comforts – a normal bed and more importantly, a normal toilet. He couldn't stand the thought of emptying a plastic box of someone else's No 1's and No 2's!

"Well your loss mate. Soon we'll be living it large! I tell you, get that bank to offer you a nice redundancy package and get yourself out of all that nonsense. Life's for living and you can't take it with yer!"

Colin smiled. Deep down that's exactly what he wanted. The rat race was, well, full of rats, and he wanted out. Trouble was they weren't in the same place as Geoff and Janice and the bank had helped them to borrow more and more to do up their house. While the staff mortgage subsidy was nice, it meant they both needed to work for a good while longer before they could make a break for freedom.

"One day, buddy, one day," he said as Pat called him to start on his first task of the day.

Chapter 4

As Geoff turned to go back indoors to see if Janice had reached the final layer of makeup, Gail came bursting out of the door. "Bye dad, just off to meet Chesney, he's really upset and needs a shoulder."

"Oh really? So that dance routine in the kitchen was you coming out in sympathy was it?" "Just remember when I was your age…"

"Daaaaad! You have no idea how relationships work these days. I was watching this YouTuber called Black Widow and she did a tutorial on how to get your man in three easy steps. Step 1 – seize the opportunity! Catch them when they are at their most vulnerable!"

"Good grief," gasped Geoff. "I dread to think what steps 2 and 3 are."

"No time now dad, I'll tell yer later or I'll miss the bus, you've a lot to learn!" And with that she raced down the avenue checking her phone app as the arrival time of the bus loomed.

Geoff had barely entered the hallway when Janice came stomping down the stairs.

"Peach melba? Who the hell decided to call it peach melba? And don't you say anything. Twenty quid this was so I'm wearing it."

As Janice got to the bottom of the stairs, he began to realise what his beloved was ranting about. Janice's face had turned a strange orange colour and his mind wandered to an old TV advert of a bald chubby bloke covered in orange slapping people in the face.

"Ha ha!" he said "You've been tangoed!"

Janice slapped him on the arm. "I said don't say anything! It's supposed to bring out the subtle peachiness and smoothness of my skin and is full of hyperallosomethingorother," she proclaimed, squinting at the minute writing on the tiny tube she held up to her eyes. "Anyway, it looks better than the fake tan Sheila at No 9 has got!"

"Hang on. Twenty quid? For that? They saw you coming! Bloody 'ell, at least you won't need that when we're wild camping."

"Yes I will!" shouted Janice. "It says it works best when you are in the outdoors as the glycowhatsit reacts with the clean air to straighten out your wrinkles naturally." As she spoke, Janice caught her reflection in the small mirror at the bottom of the stairs and proceeded to turn her head from side to side, contemplating whether it had already started to reverse the ageing process.

Geoff sighed. "Well, at least it won't weigh much. We have to keep an eye on the payload you know."

"What are you on about man. I've lost nearly 5 lbs on my *'if she can, anyone can'* diet."

Geoff was going to explain but decided better of it. And

with a toned down sigh, he grabbed the tickets he'd left on the hall table last night in readiness for the big occasion and shouted Mabel. She came scurrying out of the kitchen with her orange ball grasped tightly in her mouth, ready for anything that involved someone throwing it for the rest of the day. She dropped it on the floor and shouted "Ball field, field ball, ball field, field ball," as eloquently as she could.

"No Mabel, stop barking like that, we're not going out to play." Geoff asserted. "You're going to help us choose our motorhome! They'll be your holidays as much as ours so your need to tell us which one you like best."

Mabel's ears dropped and she took a final glance at her orange round friend. "What's the point in telling him? He doesn't listen!"

Janice locked the front door and Geoff unlocked the car. Mabel jumped in the boot when it automatically rose after Geoff had pressed the button on his key fob. He was very impressed with that feature and looked around to see if any of the neighbours had witnessed the moment. Sadly no, so he and Janice got in, belted up and he started the engine.

"Got the tickets?" Janice said. "Remember when we were going to see the Rocky Horror Picture Show in Sheffield and you forgot them. You didn't realise until we got to the place and…"

"No that wasn't Rocky Horror, it was Fleetwood Mac and it was in Leeds, at the Arena, remember? You had a dodgy belly after a curry the night before from that new takeaway and we had to stop three times on the way. They wouldn't even let you in for a final download! No, Rocky Horror was when we got there and it was the wrong day on the tickets."

"It was the right day on the tickets. It was you who put it on the wrong day on the calendar. How embarrassing when we got there and it was the first night of Swan Lake and there's you and me dressed as Frank N Furter and Riff Raff. That woman at the ticket booth nearly had kittens. It was bad enough stopping at the petrol station on the way because someone hadn't filled the car and we were on fumes! The bloke in there gave you his number and said he was free on Tuesday."

"I know. I could have swung for him. And my stockings got laddered! Still, when we did go on the right night it was awesome, eh babe?"

"Too right Franky!" said Janice with a wink. "I think we might have to get the outfits down from the loft when Gail stops over at Megan's again." She squeezed his thigh and winked again.

Geoff suddenly felt a burning sensation in his throat and let out an almighty cough, followed by another, leading to Janice snapping out of her trance.

"Anyway, we're gonna be late if we don't get a move on," Geoff croaked out when he'd got his breath back. He checked his mirror and began to reverse.

"Just watch out," warned Janice before the car had moved two metres. "You remember what happened with Colin!"

Geoff sighed again, this time more heavily. He dreamed of the day he could reverse without being reminded of 'that incident'. He safely manoeuvred out of the drive and headed down Sycamore Avenue.

He was on his way. "Soon we'll be motoring," he thought.

Chapter 5

After twenty minutes of carpool karaoke to Absolute 80s, Geoff turned down the radio as they approached the Beddleford Motor Auction Centre. He slowed down and joined a line of traffic headed the same way.

"Who would have thought it? The Motorhome Show coming to Beddleford. Mind you the Auction Centre makes a good venue. They used to hold speedway competitions here in the 1980s until one rider went through the crash barriers and up a trailer ramp they'd left out. Can't believe he cleared three Ford Escorts before he landed in that pile of tyres. I think Evil Knievel wrote to him you know, said he could switch to be a stunt rider. Wonder if he ever did?"

"Where have all these people come from?" exclaimed Janice ignoring Geoff's recollections. "Anyone would think it was free entry! Look there, that man is waving people into that bit."

Geoff pulled into the space indicated by the parking guy and turned off the engine. "We're here babe, we're really here! By the end of the day we'll have our very own motorhome, just what we've dreamed of!"

"I know, I'm starting to get a bit tingly now. But remember, we've got a budget and we're sticking to it. We know which one we want and we just need to get the best price."

Geoff and Janice had signed up to a monthly magazine a year ago and had scoured the 'expert reviews' to find the motorhome of their dreams. And eventually, they had seen it. A nice four berth with all the space Janice wanted plus the vanity mirror in the bathroom, and all the 'mod cons' Geoff wanted.

"Yeh I know," said Geoff. "But you never know."

Janice rolled her eyes. She knew what Geoff was like. When they went to get their latest car, they'd agreed on a nice little four door. Why not, as there was only the three of them and Gail hardly came out with them now. Mabel could get in the boot, nice and economical, all sorted. They left having signed up for the 4x4 that brought them here. Geoff said it was the panoramic sunroof and the auto opening boot that were a 'must have' these days. The salesman must have thought it was the easiest sell ever. Janice hoped for a miracle today.

They got Mabel out of the boot, Geoff taking a quick glance around as the boot smoothly opened and closed without him touching it. No, bad timing, no one seemed to see, but if they had, they'd have made it a 'must have' when they got their next car, he thought.

They got to the entrance and Geoff proudly presented his tickets. The man on the door was dressed in a black suit and looked like he should be working outside "Big Dave's" nightclub in town.

"Sorry mate. Can't come in with these tickets."

Geoff's jaw dropped and he felt himself glance at his feet as if he'd been told his trainers were too green.

"What do you mean?" he said as Janice prepared herself for battle.

"These tickets are for tomorrow. You've paid for these because tomorrow is when the entertainment is on. Woodfleet Mac – tribute band and all that."

Janice looked at Geoff and adjusted her attack position forty five degrees to face him. "You idiot! Can't you ever buy the right tickets?!"

"Don't worry love," said the bouncer "You can go in as it's free today. You just can't come in using these tickets."

Geoff turned to look behind him at the queue that was building up and was sure he heard a ripple of sniggers but couldn't quite tell from whom. He grabbed the tickets from the doorman who was also trying to stop himself from busting into laughter.

"Well, we planned to come tomorrow as well, we're massive Fleetwood Mac fans, seen them loads of times!" Geoff said smugly. " Come on Janice, we've got a pension to spend!"

And he marched in pulling Mabel along beside, which she thoroughly resented as she'd found some chips on the ground and had nearly finished cleaning them up.

As they entered the auction house, they were aghast at how it had been transformed into a showroom of gleaming chariots, all different shapes and sizes, just waiting to entice them inside. Above their heads, huge signs displayed the different makes and models with flashy banners offering ten or fifteen percent off the RRP! There was a low hum of lots of conversations as couples, families and friends discussed the pros and cons of each one, sometimes heightened with an "ooohh that's amazing" or "aahhh that's a must have" and even a "how much??"

"Ok Geoff, grab a map from that stall over there and let's get to the one we want."

Geoff didn't answer. Janice looked across at him and saw a glazed look across his face and his mouth open wide. She could have sworn she saw a drop of saliva form on his bottom lip. The last time she had seen him like that was when they went to the Beddlesford Roxy to see Pretty Woman in the 1980s and Julia Roberts had walked on screen in thigh length boots.

"Twice he dropped buttered popcorn down his shirt," she thought "and that butter stain never did come out!"

"Geoff!" she shouted and Mabel spun round and sat down abruptly. When mum shouted like that she knew someone was going to get it and if she behaved like one of those dogs in the box in the living room that chases sheep, she'd be ok. They always got a cuddle in the end and most of the time they sat or lay down immediately when the man with the hat shouted.

"Would you look at that!" Geoff said, wiping his mouth on his sleeve. "I've died and gone to heaven."

"It might be sooner than you think," said Janice. "Just get a map and let's find the one we want".

"But Janice, I never realised there were this many. Maybe we've been a bit hasty. That magazine didn't have all these models, maybe we'll find an even better one!"

Janice looked up to the heavens and wondered what it would look like with Geoff up there sitting on a cloud, playing his harp. Mabel sat very still. She could see mum's face turn that strange colour that happened either when someone was going to get it or when she said her food was too spicy.

"I've spent a whole year listening to you read those bloody magazines from cover to cover. Every make, model, trip, complaint and technical toilet issue! I know how to put an extra leisure battery in, how to change a rusty exhaust and where to find my inverter!! We are getting the one we said!!"

"Ok, ok, calm down, calm down" said Geoff in a mildly recognisable Scouse accent and waving his hands up and down.

"Harry Enfield would be proud," he thought. Mabel looked at Geoff and then at Janice. She knew that was a bad move and stayed very still.

"Think you're a funny man?" Janice growled in an equally vague Irish accent that seemed to come from nowhere. She grabbed a map and slapped him on the head.

Mabel sighed in relief. "Not me this time" she thought. "Must remember to pay attention to the dogs in the box to learn more ways to become invisible when the shouting starts."

Geoff laughed. Janice and he could always diffuse their tempers with a quick character change.

"Who would have the best accent? Me!" he thought, but he had to admit Janice's Irish accent was better than his.

"Come on then, let's find it." He took the map and unfolded it. " Bloody 'ell. This is like a maze!" He scoured the map which had now unfolded to the size of a Sunday newspaper, the proper ones with all the supplements and magazines, not the red top ones. "It's all just coloured dots with numbers and letters on. How are you supposed to find anything?"

Janice rolled her eyes. "You look on the other side and find the name of the make and then look down the list of models – each one has got a reference against it. Good grief man, did you get any O'Levels?"

"Well that's bad design that is, you have to keep turning it over. A bloke could get lost in here forever!"

"You wish," said Janice and ran her finger down the make they wanted – Phoenix was the make – she liked that because it reminded her of River Phoenix the actor. Wouldn't kick him out for farting, that's for sure!

"There," she said when she had recovered her senses. "Phoenix Crusader, it's on aisle number 12, plot G7. Easy when you know how," and turned her hand into the shape of a gun and blew the top of her finger. "Just like River Phoenix," she thought "or was it Clint Eastwood?"

"Well it's scientifically proven men can't do two things at once," said Geoff turning the map over and over, trying to remember the reference and then pinpoint it on the other side. "Women have different hormones or enzymes or something that we haven't got."

"Well, if you could do one thing at once, it would be a miracle." she said taking Mabel's lead from Geoff as she sniffed underneath the map stand. Mabel was sure there was another chip under the stand and the smell made her think it must be a big one. She edged her nose underneath and there it was, big and chunky and covered in that red sauce dad puts all over his chips.

She'd tasted that and liked it and she now began to get

excited at the prospect of devouring this huge chip. She scurried under the stall and was inches away from it. Her tongue, which could enter the Guinness Book of Records for the longest ever, lapped towards her prize when all of a sudden she heard "Mabel!!" and with that she tried to get up and sit like the dogs in the box had taught her.

As she rose up, Mabel tipped the stall over and all the maps tumbled onto the floor. The stall came down with an almighty crash and Mabel, who now realised that her plan had not worked, ran around Geoff looking for cover from mum. As the lead tightened around his legs, Geoff realised he was shortly going to lose his balance and reached out for something, anything to stabilise himself. The only thing within his grasp was Janice and he grabbed for her arm.

In an instant, Geoff and Janice fell to the ground like a sad parody of Torvill and Dean at the end of their Bolero gold medal performance, except Janice landed face down onto Geoff's crotch rather than gracefully at his side. As Geoff fell, the lead tightened even more and Mabel also found herself being dragged down on top of the tangle of arms and legs that were her mum and dad.

The people around them, including the bouncer from Big Dave's burst into laughter, pointing at the carnage on the floor at the entrance to the show.

Mabel, realising she may have played a small part in the calamity, jumped on Janice licking her face for all she was worth.

"Gerroff!" shouted Janice. "Your breath smells of raw duck!" Mabel decided to help dad instead but found the lead wasn't long enough to reach his face. "She's cutting off the blood to my legs!" Geoff shouted as the lead got tighter and tighter as Mabel tried harder and harder to reach him, her tongue stretching out like one of those lizards you see on David Attenborough.

Bouncer Dave *[we'll call him that now]* decided he would use his position of authority to take charge of the situation and took the lead handle from Janice's hand. As he did, Mabel spotted the chip she had been after just behind Geoff's head and made one almighty leap for it. She was deceptively strong for her size and as she launched forward, Dave felt the tug on his end of the lead and fell forwards on top of Janice.

Janice, now effectively the middle of a man sandwich, tried to scream but found no sound would come out. Geoff was now unsure whether his life was going to end through loss of blood to his legs or from being squashed by his wife and Bouncer Dave. It wasn't how he'd envisaged it all ending.

Thankfully, Mabel got enough slack from Bouncer Dave's fall to reach the chip and gobbled it up in an instant. She crawled back over Geoff's head just as Bouncer Dave let go of the lead. This freed him to get to his feet and help Janice up. Janice was stunned. Never before had she been wedged between two men on the floor and she wasn't entirely sure what thoughts were going through her mind. She shook her head and dusted herself down.

"Get up man, everybody's staring!" she scowled. Geoff rolled over to untangle the lead from his legs and put his hands down to raise himself up. As he got to his feet he felt a warmth on his left hand and looked down to see it was covered in tomato sauce and the remnants of another squashed chunky chip.

"Uuurrgghh!" he exclaimed as Mabel leapt up and licked his hand clean. "Have you brought the baby wipes Janice?"

Janice put her head in her hands. Why did it always happen to her. This was the man she was going to spend the rest of her life with, most of the time in a tin box in the middle of nowhere. She should have listened to her mother.

"I knew you were trouble when you came in," said Bouncer Dave picking up the map stall and stacking the maps back in. "First you try and con your way in and now you're smashing the place up. I'm keeping my eye on you mate so watch it!"

Geoff sighed one of his deep sighs. This was not how he had planned it. With the show over, the crowd dispersed and Geoff and Janice made their way to aisle 12, G7, with a very content Mabel trotting behind, licking a stray bit of red sauce from the side of her mouth.

Chapter 6

As they walked down the walkways towards aisle 12, Geoff and Janice gazed at the new gleaming motorhomes on either side. Prospective buyers were swarming like bees, inside and outside the vehicles, as company reps clamoured to hand out brochures and answer questions. Streamline coach builts, traditional Lutons, van conversions, you name it, they were here, in all their glory.

As they past one on the left, a rep began to disperse the spectators hovering around the side. "Stand aside, stand aside please," he said with a certain authority that could have come from Bouncer Dave.

"Ok Bob," he shouted.

Bob, who was somewhere inside the vehicle, must have done something as all of a sudden the side of the motorhome began to move with a soothing hum.

"Oooohs" and "Aaaaahs" began to ripple through the crowd, which was beginning to swell now. The side continued to glide outwards for another few feet until it clicked to a stop.

"Will you look at that Janice" said Geoff. "Imagine rolling up at Whitby in this!"

Janice had to admit she was impressed. She began thinking about parking up on the clifftop near Whitby Abbey, their favourite place, and taking walks along the sea front with Mabel. She peered through the window and saw a couple chatting and smiling, presumably the ones who had asked for the demo that had impressed everyone.

"One day that will be us Geoff!" she said and squeezed his hand.

"You're not wrong Janice, you're not wrong! Come on Mabel, our carriage awaits." And with that they continued their journey.

"Here we go," said Janice. "Aisle 12". They walked down as Geoff counted "G2, 3 , 4…there it is! Janice there it is!"

There in G7 stood the magnificent Phoenix Crusader Mark III. Geoff handed Mabel's lead to Janice and leapt towards his dream 'home from home'.

"Don't run man! It's not going anywhere!" shouted Janice and then smiled as she saw her man dance a gig like the one he told her about when he was 8 years old and got a Raleigh Chopper on Christmas Day.

Mabel, seeing her dad perform his second strange dance of the day, tugged on her lead to go check he was ok. The last time he ended up on the kitchen floor and she knew her kisses made him feel better.

"Ok Mabel, mummy's coming," said Janice as she broke into a jog.

By now Geoff had opened the habitation door *[that's a technical term for the, well door]*. He ran his hand down the chrome handle on the inside, opened the attached waste bin *[presumably to check it was empty]* and then climbed the small step into his castle.

Janice followed with Mabel, who thought this was an exciting new adventure with places she was sure to find a chip, maybe with some of that red stuff on.

"Janice look!" exclaimed Geoff, "It's just like the one in the magazine!"

"It is the one in the magazine man. We decided on this model!"

"I know, but isn't it so much better in real life? Smell that newness, you don't get that second hand." Geoff had turned left through the *[habitation]* door and was standing in a front living area where there was seating for four people with a table.

"Look at the space. We can easily get us all in here and even Colin and Pat if we can ever persuade them to see the light!" Geoff said as he ran his hand over the seats and sat down as if preparing himself for his next meal to be served.

"Hang on Geoff. Let's just enjoy it ourselves first, get used to it, you know. This is our time to relax. I'm not spending time entertaining while you go off fishing!"

Janice looked up and saw the overhead *[another technical term]* cupboards. "Ooh these are nice," she said clicking open the button and watching as the cupboard door slowly rose up revealing a very spacious interior. " I can get loads in there."

"Ok but don't go mad, remember the MUP," Geoff said, feeling very proud of himself to have remembered the acronym. *[Apologies for more technical stuff but owning a motorhome gets very technical. MUP is Maximum User*

Payload to you and me, it means how much the things you put inside can weigh before the vehicle, well, falls over I guess. They never really tell you what happens if you go over. I must check into that...]

"Yeh, whatever" said Janice. "That's your department. I just want to make sure I get my nice new dinner set in there for our Al Fresco dining."

"Al who? Is he another of those Chefs on telly? I don't want any poncy food while we're away Janice. BBQs all round for me!"

Janice rolled her eyes and laughed. Geoff was not a big fan of fine cuisine and that was ok with Janice as she liked to cook proper food that made you feel sleepy.

"Don't worry, I've not got his cookery book," she said smiling.

They walked back through the cabin to the kitchen area and Janice was very pleased with what she saw. Lots of space *[she is a bit claustrophobic]* and more cupboard space, just where she needs it.

"A proper oven" Janice thought. "Not like the European ones, they don't seem to need four rings for some reason. Maybe they don't eat enough veg." Her eyes panned to the nice chrome sink, worktop space and underneath an integral fridge, which she opened to find a small freezer in the top half.

"That'll do nicely," she thought. She opened the drawer above the fridge and took a sigh of relief. A cutlery drawer with a cutlery holder! "You can never find one to fit so that's good," said Janice turning to see where Geoff was.

Opposite the kitchen area was a door which was open and Geoff was inside pretending to have a shower.

"Look Janice, plenty of room in here for me! We could both get in together," Geoff proclaimed with a wink.

"You must be joking man!" exclaimed Janice. "I'll be in the facilities, they have nice and hot showers and some even have Dyson hairdryers. It was in the April magazine."

Geoff finished his pretend shower and checked the washbasin and toilet. "Very nice, very nice" he said. "We'll be made up in here. Nothing to want for."

By now Mable had got a bit bored as there were no morsels to be found and the funny smell she encountered when she first jumped in wasn't very appetising. She pulled Janice into the rear of the motorhome where there was a U shaped lounge. *[Now you can get all sorts of different shapes and sizes to the lounge area in a motorhome but Janice had insisted on one with a U shape. It's the space, less claustrophobic you see and the seats convert into a double bed – very practical!].*

" Now this is what it's all about," she said and sat down on the sofa that cured round the end of the van. "I can stretch out here and read my book in peace and quiet."

"And I can watch the telly on this side," said Geoff as he lay down on the opposite sofa and gazed at the tv bracket on the wall. "I can just see a nice 22 inch on there with a built in DVD. Or we can get one of those firestick thingys that Colin's got. He says he can get everything on that. Amazing cos it's tiny!"

Mabel saw mummy sitting down as a cue to jump up for a lap cuddle. This was the routine at home every weeknight after tea time and just when the programme started when Geoff, Janice and Gail all sang "One! de de dat dat de de, One! de de dat dat de de, One!" for some reason.

"Get down Mabel. Not until it's ours!"

"Yes get down Mabel, the man's coming." Geoff shouted. "Look Janice, here's the rep, get her down and let's get sorted."

Chapter 7

A bald headed man with a smart white shirt and blue tie stepped up into the cabin. His smile reminded Janice of the Cheshire cat in Alice In Wonderland and she now had visions of Geoff as the Mad Hatter.

"Hello, hello" said the man, "I'm Stuart and I can see you are admiring the Crusader III, the latest in British design and technology, built with you in mind because we…errm, we mind about you."

Stuart hadn't been a motorhome sales rep for very long, in fact this was his first day. He stuttered a little to remember the last bit of the opening lines he'd practised over and over last night but he'd got there and the clients didn't seem to notice.

"Hello Stuart. I'm Geoff and this is my better half Janice. And this is Mabel, don't worry, she harmless enough, unless you deliver takeaway leaflets, for some reason she just doesn't like them."

"How lovely" said Stuart, nervously smiling at Mabel, who was wondering whether the paperwork in his hands were leaflets or not.

Stuart wasn't a big fan of dogs. He thinks it stems back to when he was 10 years old and he'd bought a 99 cone from the ice cream van in Bridlington. A German Shepherd had sneaked up on him and snatched it out of his hand before he got a lick. He'd never felt safe around dogs since and, come to that, never bought a 99 cone again.

"Maybe if you just shorten his lead a bit?" he said biting his lip and squeezing his clipboard until his knuckles turned a brilliant white colour.

"Mabel, come here!" shouted Geoff "It's a she but she's a tough 'un. Don't let her size deceive you!"

"Oh, I won't" said Stuart, relaxing the muscles that had now tensed throughout his body. He took a seat next to Janice and felt more reassured that she was between him and the dog.

"So are we just browsing today? Is the Crusader Mark III something you've had your eye on?" Stuart remembered his training not to go in too hard early on. They say your first sale is your hardest so he would ease the conversation slowly. He really needed to impress his boss Mr Payne today to get his probationary period off to a good start.

"Where do we sign errrr, Stuart?" said Geoff eagerly, squinting to see the name badge that was pinned on Stuart's crisp white shirt.

"Oh, well, are you sure? There are many models and variations in the Crusader series. Perhaps if I show you the key features…" He felt day three of his training returning in a flash. "Make sure you find the thing that will 'nail the sale' – that's what Mr Payne had said on day three" he thought.

"No you're alright" said Geoff. "We know what we want, don't we Janice? Been researching for a year now. I could tell you everything about this beauty if you like. Height 2.82 metres, 2.3 litre Ducati engine, 4 berth including electric drop down bed for maximum comfort and space saving. Truma heating system with a 100 litre fresh water tank, twin gas…"

"Alright Geoff. Good grief, you'd think he'd swallowed the manual! It's ok Stu, can I call you Stu? We came today to buy this one and believe me, my husband has been like an expectant father for weeks so we won't make it difficult for you today. You can save your sales pitch for another customer."

Stuart felt a little faint. Day 3 training flashed before him and he couldn't see the module on 'When customers make it easy'.

"Errm, well ok. If you're sure Mr and Mrs…?"

"Watt" said Janice.

"Eh, your name? Mr and Mrs…?"

"Watt, that's our name. With no 'h' and two Ts Stu. We're not American you know. But you can call us Geoff and Janice, nice and friendly."

"Yes, quite" said Stuart. "Well, Mr and…Geoff and Janice, I'll just need to complete some details and go through the payment terms and Bob's your uncle!"

"I think you'll find Bob down at that mega motorhome with the sliding walls" chuckled Geoff. " But I did have an Uncle Bob, he used to be an ice cream man, Ice Cream Bob he was called. Best Mr Whippy in town."

"Err, yes quite" said Stuart, remembering again his childhood encounter with an ice cream and he looked nervously at Mabel, who was now certain she could smell something tasty on the bottom of Stuart's shoe. She started to pull on the lead and sniff towards his leg.

"I'll be back in a jiffy" said Stuart as he quickly got up and headed for the habitation door *[that's the door that takes you outside – keep up!]*.

"I'll get the paperwork ready out here and bring it all in to sign." And with that he was gone.

"Bit edgy, isn't he?" said Geoff.

"I think he's new" said Janice, "you can always tell. Did you see his neck? All red, that's a sign he was nervous. My mother used to say never go out with a lad with a red neck."

Mabel was disappointed that she didn't get to explore the tall man's shoe. She was sure she'd smelled a bit of that red sauce and spotted a bit of chip on the sole.

'Oh well, next time,' she thought. 'I do need a wee though. Not much grass around here.'

"Can you believe it?" said Geoff. "We're really going to own all this." He gazed around the cabin like a king surveying his castle. "This is it Janice. This is the life we've been waiting for. Living the dream we said and living the dream we'll do!"

"Oh Geoff, I can't wait until we are pitched up sat outside with a glass of Pinot and you've got the BBQ going. Then off for a long walk with Mabel, breathing all that fresh air! I love you darling."

And with that Janice leaned forward to Geoff and gave him their customary three quick kisses on the lips.

"I love you too gorgeous" crooned Geoff and then they both sat silently and dreamily imagining what adventures lay ahead.

Mabel looked at dad and then mum and had seen that look before. She decided to lie down because sometimes that took away the need to wee for a while. She curled up on Geoff's feet and closed her eyes. She felt good about this little house, she could get used to this.

A few minutes later, Stuart returned with a pile of papers and edged his way to sit next to Janice. Mabel woke with a jump, opened her eyes and spotted an intruder coming towards her. She leapt to her feet barking madly. If anyone was going to burgle their house, they'd have to get past her first.

"Mabel pack it in. It's only Stu." said Janice. "Take Mabel over your side." She handed Geoff the lead and mouthed silently, "I think Stu has stood in something" and her eyes turned to look at Stuart's feet.

Geoff understood and took Mabel and shortened her lead so she had no room to manoeuvre towards the tall man with the interesting foot. Mabel came to her senses and realised it was the man with the tasty shoe. She looked again and yes, there it was, some red stuff. She decided to wait for her moment and sat very obediently next to Geoff. She really did need a wee.

Stuart sat down tentatively, "Nice doggy" he said. "I'm a cat person myself. Find they don't like ice cream." Janice and Geoff looked at each other thoughtfully.

Ten minutes later and Stuart proclaimed "So, if you just sign one more time here" watching as Geoff and then Janice added their signatures to the final form, "and we are all done. You are now the proud owners of the Phoenix Crusader Mark III. And may I say, you have made the perfect choice."

Stuart had already calculated his commission and couldn't wait to tell Mr Payne on his next tea break.

"Thank you Stu" said Janice. "We are so excited, aren't we Geoff?"

"Oh Stu, you have changed our lives. This is my dream, mate. You have no idea how long I've waited to have one of these. We are going to explore the world!"

"Well, let's start somewhere closer to home love" said Janice, bringing him back down to earth, well most likely the Lake District to be precise. "Then we'll see."

"Well, enjoy!" said Stuart and rose to leave them to dream a bit more.

"We have an exclusive offer at the show today. Your vehicle will be delivered to your house, not a usual service but we're trialling it out. How does Wednesday suit you? We just need a few days to give it the once over and make sure everything is tip top!"

Geoff looked at Janice. "Hey love, imagine our new motorhome pulling up in Sycamore Avenue, all shiny and new! Colin will be out like a shot!"

"Wednesday's perfect" said Janice. "I'll need to weed the front garden."

Stuart looked bemused but quickly put the thought out of his head and stood up.

Mabel realised the tall man was going to leave. She figured dad had been sat a long time holding her lead and the chances were he'd loosened his grip. She leapt forward, tongue out, desperate to get a taste of that red sauce again. Stuart saw Mabel out of the corner of his eye and he suddenly had that ratatouille moment *[you know the one where you get transported back to a time in your childhood. Well if you've not seen the film, watch it, then you'll get it].*

Mabel was now a German Shepherd hurtling towards his ice cream. Stuart let out the wail of a 10 year old about to lose his 99 and ran down the cabin and out of the door.

"Mabel, leave the man alone" said Geoff.

Mabel sighed. No more sauce and she was now desperate for a wee. She ran to mummy and leapt up at her, burrowing her head in her lap.

"I think she needs a wee," said Janice. "I can always tell."

Mabel heard mum say that word "wee" and began licking her hand.

"Told you" said Janice and stood up. "Listen, I'll find somewhere to have a wee and you have a little look round. I'll meet you back at the map stand."

"Ok love" said Geoff. He was thinking about his new baby arriving in just four days' time. As it pulled up in front of the drive, Colin and the other neighbours would be peeping out of their curtains, gasping in amazement. At last, he would be the talk of the avenue, but this time in a good way.

They would forget the time he caused a power cut in the whole street when he tried to fit an outside plug for his ornamental waterfall. Four hours everyone had no power and it didn't help when that idiot from the electricity board went round and told people what he'd done. "A right comic he was (not)!" Geoff thought.

"Pass me the map and I'll meet you in 10 minutes".

Chapter 8

Geoff stood outside G7 and looked at the map.
"Who the 'ell designed this?" he said to himself under his breath. "Where are the toilets? I could do with a wee now after all that excitement. I know how Mabel feels."

He looked for the public convenience sign on the map. "Oh no, it's back down near the entrance." He thought. "I may as well go on the way out to meet Janice. Hey, I wonder if they've got that rock bus that was in the last magazine? What was it called? Gladiator was it?"

He scanned down the names as Janice had shown him and sure enough, there it was. Aisle 11, C2. "Aisle 11, that's just next door" Geoff thought. "I'll just have a quick peek and then go meet Janice."

He made his way to the end of aisle 12 and turned left into aisle 11. He walked a few yards forward and then stopped in his tracks.

"Bloomin' 'eck!" he said out loud. "What a beauty! You could get two of ours into that thing. I remember seeing one like this when we went looking for Stevie Nicks after that Fleetwood Mac gig. Never did get her signature but what a bus!"

In front of him rose a silver and black touring bus, around 11 metres long with blacked out windows and chrome shining everywhere. Along the side were the words *Gladiator 1000* in embossed silver lettering.

Geoff looked around and was shocked to see no one was taking much interest at the moment. He approached the side entrance and saw a sign saying "next viewings at 12pm." He looked at his Fitbit. "11.45, I reckon I could just sneak in for a minute or two, no harm done." He thought. Geoff glanced around, happy no one was paying any attention to plot C2.

He went to the door and saw a push button with 'open' written above. He pressed the button and the door moved outwards a little and then to the side with a swish. "Just like on Star Trek" thought Geoff. "Captain Geoff T Watt coming aboard!" Geoff didn't have a middle name but if he had, he would have wanted it to be Tiberius.

He stepped up into the cabin, or better to say the lounge as it opened out into a lavish sitting room with velvet sofas with a marble looking coffee table in the middle. Above hung a small chandelier and all around the walls were glass fronted cupboards. He panned further left and saw a fully fitted kitchen with a built in dishwasher and washing machine. To the right he stepped forward into a master bedroom with a four poster bed and more crystal lights. Opening a door to the right of the bed he came across a walk in wardrobe with shoe rack and trouser press. "Who uses a trouser press?" he thought.

He saw another door beyond the bed and decided to explore further. Captain Watt was on a mission now. He opened the door and found himself in the most luxurious bathroom he had ever seen, even better than the one they had in that hotel in Lanzarote where he and Janice went for their anniversary last year.

"Unbelievable!" Geoff thought. "This is classy. A full size bath! Janice would love that. Glass of wine and one of those romance books! One day Janice, one day!" Next to the bath was a walk in shower, one of those with the wall mounted jet wash shower that sprayed water from top to toe – amazing! "And look at that! A proper lav! With a flush and everything!"

All of a sudden, Geoff felt that feeling you get when you hit your 50s. When what was a mild need for a wee turns into a desperate need to go. He had forgotten about his urge to wee when he'd left Janice and now it had crept up on him with a vengeance. Geoff knew he was 5 minutes from the entrance. He'd never make it.

He looked at the lav again. "No one will know" he thought. He went over to the marble toilet and lifted the lid. Now men of a certain age know they have to sit down to get the full benefits of a successful wee so he prepared himself and sat down. In an instant, he began to sigh as this morning's black coffee bid him farewell.

He looked across into the mirror on the wall opposite and saw his face relax. Who would believe it? He's sat having a wee in the new *Gladiator 1000!* Feeling proud of himself, he stood up, dressed himself, and turned to flush the loo. "Oh I wonder if they've plumbed it in?" he thought. "Well, we'll soon find out." And with that he pressed the button on the top of the toilet. There was a whoosh as blue fluid sprayed automatically from inside the bowl and somewhere below sucked all the water out of the pan, followed by a gurgling noise as water began to return into it.

"Now that's impressive!" said Geoff. "You don't even get that power from our one at home!"

Geoff began to turn away when he noticed the water was still filling up the toilet bowl. He watched as it became about half full and water continued to pump in.

"Hang on, that's not right," he said and pressed the flush button a few times in quick succession. That only seemed to encourage more water to pump into the bowl and accelerate the level towards the top.

"Oh 'eck!" said Geoff. He looked around and saw a set of twin towels with 'him' and 'her' draped over a gold radiator. He thought about the little boy and the dam and figured it was worth a go.

"That ought to do the trick," he thought. "After all that lad turned out to be famous didn't he?" He pushed one of the towels down into the toilet and stood back. All of a sudden the sucking mechanism he had heard earlier started again and the towel slowly started disappearing down the pipe. He waited. Another gurgling sound began and then a whirring, like you hear when your electric toothbrush is charging down.

"That's the ticket!" said Geoff.

Bang! Bang bang! The towel had now disappeared altogether and the water began filling again, only faster now. Geoff heard more water, this time coming from the marble sink.

"What the…" he shouted.

Water began to emerge from the sink plughole and the basin began to fill, faster than the toilet bowl.

"Oh no!" screamed Geoff and put his hands over the plug hole in the sink.

The water pressure was now increasing so fast it began spraying between his fingers soaking his shirt and his face. He took his hands away just as the toilet bowl began to over flow. At that same moment there was another bang, probably as the towel made its way through the sophisticated pumping system under the floor. Just then the shower decided to join the party and streams of water began jetting out of all the holes. It didn't take long for the shower enclosure to start filling up too.

"This can't be happening" cried Geoff, now starting to realise the enormity of what was unfolding before his eyes.

Chapter 9

His feet were now soaking as the water on the floor got deeper. He took the remaining towel and tried to mop up what he could, but the hole in the dam was getting bigger and bigger. He looked at his watch.

"11.55, I need to get out of here," he muttered to himself. Geoff turned just as the shower door flung open under the weight of the gallons of water that had accumulated in just a minute or so.

As he turned the rushing water lifted him clean off his feet and he fell to the floor with a thump. Geoff looked up to see the ceiling was all mirrored and for a brief second thought that looked a bit tacky for such a classy van! He then regained his senses as he realised his back was soaked through and the water was now inches deep. He got up and opened the bathroom door. He leapt into the bedroom followed by a torrent of water. He felt like he'd jumped from Star Trek to Indiana Jones in one moment and ran to the habitation door *[yep the exit]*.

Geoff looked out of the window next to the door and saw a very smartly dressed rep just passing C5 and heading his way. He could see a *Gladiator* branded clipboard in his hand and that he walked with an air of someone who constantly smelled something bad.

"Oh 'eck, no way out there," Geoff deduced.

He ran back into the bedroom and spotted a window on the far wall *[so the opposite side from the habitation door – still with me?]*

He was relieved to see they were not radio controlled, just the old fashioned levers, and pulled them up and tried to open it as fully as he could. *[Now motorhome windows open on a hydraulic piston and usually have two opening settings – a bit and a lot – and you need to jiggle it a bit to find the catch that keeps it open.]*

Try as he might, Geoff couldn't find the catch and, seeing the window was wide but not tall, decided he had to just go for it. With water now over his feet in the bedroom, he climbed onto the ornate bedside table, kicked over the crystal lamp with the gold cherub holding it up, curled up his legs and rolled himself through the window. What he'd forgotten was how high up he was.

He landed with a thump on the artificial grass that surrounded all the motorhomes – gave it an outdoorsy feeling which was nice.

Geoff scrambled to his knees just as he heard the *Gladiator* rep open the *[you know what]* door. Geoff peered in the window just in time to see a flood of water crash over the bottom of the rep's legs and continue to pour out in a fashion that reminded Geoff of his visit to Niagara Falls in 1984.

Without further ado, he turned and weaved his way between two small campervans back into aisle 11. The high pitched screams of the rep rang in his ears as he pulled the soggy map from the back of his jeans to check where the entrance was.

Chapter 10

Geoff found his way towards the entrance more easily than he imagined and there at the map stand was Janice and Mabel. He looked at his watch – 12.05 – that was close!

"Ok, ready to go now," said Geoff as he approached them. "Did Mabel have a wee?"

Just then there began a crescendo of noise from the arena as people began to move towards them, firstly walking quickly, and then breaking in a run, jostling elbows everywhere.

Bouncer Dave, who was still manning the entrance, held his hand to his ear and then said "Roger, got that Jim," and shouted "Right, everybody out!"

"What's going on?" said Janice to Bouncer Dave.

"We're having to evacuate. Some idiot has flooded the showcase motorhome and they can't stop the water pouring out, everywhere is flooding. Bloody nightmare! Everybody out! This way!"

"We'd better do as he says love," said Geoff tentatively to Janice.

Janice looked Geoff up and down. "Geoff, why is your hair wet? And turn round. What in bloody hell…!"

"Let's go love, nothing to see here!" And with that, Geoff grabbed Janice's hand and Mabel's lead and they headed out and off to the car.

"Don't look back Janice."

The drive home was a quiet one. Even Mabel lay down quietly in the back, quite pleased to be heading home where she didn't have to scavenge for a treat to eat.

Geoff pulled into the drive and he and Janice got out and let Mabel out of the boot. As they opened the front door they heard the TV on in the living room.

"Is that you mum? Dad?" It was Gail.

"You'll never guess what's happened! It's all over the local news. Some wally flooded the most expensive motorhome at that show you went to. Thousands of pounds damage they think. Still can't stop the water. They'd connected it to the mains and they couldn't find the stop cock or something, that bit sounded rude I thought. Anyway, had to close the whole show for the rest of the day. Can't wait 'til they get hold of whoever did that! It'll go viral!"

"No Gail" grimaced Janice as she glared at Geoff. "Neither can I!"

Geoff held his head. "Suppose we won't be going back to see Woodfleet Mac tomorrow then?"

Janice rolled her eyes. "Go get out of those wet clothes man. Your Motorhome Show days are well and truly over!"

Chapter 11

Geoff kept a low profile for the next couple of days. He only went out when he needed to and only once got caught by his neighbour Colin. He almost got back in the house after dropping an empty bran flakes box into the green bin when he heard the familiar shout.

"Alright Geoff!" Geoff turned slowly, gave a little wave and smiled. He started to turn back when he sensed Colin approaching.

"Hey, you've been quiet since you went for your campervan, err I mean motorhome. Thought you'd be over giving me the lowdown, Didn't you get it? Hey, did the place flood before you could sign up? What a disaster. I can't wait until they find who did it. They say it was sabotage, you know. Apparently they've got CCTV so shouldn't be long now. Local news say they'll tell us when they know."

Geoff winced. "CCTV, that's handy." He hadn't thought of that.

"Yeh we heard about it. I'm sure it was an accident. These things happen. But we did sign up. It comes this

Wednesday. We'll be away by the weekend, away from all this." Geoff looked around the avenue and pictured himself away from anyone who knew about the motorhome show fiasco.

"Cool. I'm working from home Wednesday so I'll keep an eye out," said Colin and glanced up to the first floor window of the bedroom he had converted into an office. I can keep an eye on all the coming and going from there. You never know who's about Geoff."

"No" sighed Geoff. "Well, I'm busy ordering some essentials on Amazon so I'll be seeing you." And with that Geoff went inside and slammed the door.

"Nice" said Colin.

[Now anyone who's bought a motorhome knows you need lots of accessories. In fact you never stop buying accessories. As soon as you think you have everything you need, you see something different or someone that has something different.]

Geoff scoured Amazon for his essentials. He'd made a list, as Janice had told him to, and now he was working his way through, adding them to his basket until he checked and saw he had 17 items waiting to checkout.

"£156.23, flaming 'ell!" shouted Geoff. "How much was that smokeless BBQ charcoal?"

"Well just make sure you've got everything we need," said Janice. I don't want to turn up there and find we don't have a cork screw!"

"Corkscrew" thought Geoff and quickly searched and found one with 2,389 five star reviews. "Blimey, £19.99! Ah well, you can't take it with you, add to basket," he said and clicked the checkout button.

"Are we all booked in then at that nice one in the Lake District? I'd have preferred Whitby as our first trip really." asked Janice.

"Yep, we're in. Whitby was fully booked love. Unless you wanted no hook up but don't fancy that until we do a bit of wild camping," said Geoff.

"Ok well, it has good reviews and they say its peaceful and relaxing, just what we need after that bloody motorhome show."

"Yes dear," replied Geoff sheepishly.

Chapter 12

Geoff's Fitbit sprang into life at 7am on Wednesday morning. He leaned over and prodded Janice. "Wake up love! Today's the day!"

Janice rolled towards him and groaned. "What time is it?"

"7am, need to get ready!"

Janice sighed. "But it's not coming until 11 man!"

"Yes, but we need to be ready love. Oh and morning Mrs W, I love you."

"Oh Geoff you idiot, I was having a great dream with him who plays Iron Man. He was rescuing me from a giant squirrel that was trying to bury me in the fig tree pot on the decking! That must be because I haven't put any nuts out for a few days. Dreams tell you things you know, I read it in 'Take A Break'. Don't know where you were! Not much chance you'd be in that suit! Oh well, morning Mr W, I love you too."

And they proceeded to complete the daily ritual with their three quick kisses and Janice wondered what delights today held in store.

In the kitchen, Geoff and Janice ate their breakfast of shreddies with some sort of fruit inside as Gail entered the room, her eyes still half closed.

"I didn't sleep a wink!" she moaned. "Chesney is thinking of giving it another go with Chelsea," she said. "After I bought him a Big Mac too."

"Well, if you can't win him with food, don't try anything else young lady!" said Janice. "When I was your age…"

"When you were my age mum, there wasn't social media! I changed my status from single to attached and now everybody thinks we're together! Tuscany is even arranging a party and everything!"

Gail had put a slice of bread in the toaster and was waiting impatiently for it to pop up.

Geoff sighed. "That Instaface should be banned," he stated with some authority. "All it brings is misery and no one even looks like themselves on there. All that face brushing!"

"Air brushing dad, it's air brushing!" Gail countered abruptly. "Anyway, I need more beauty sleep if I'm going to get him."

And with that, the toaster popped. She grabbed the hot bread gingerly and quickly put it on a plate, turned and left the room.

"Don't forget we are going away this weekend and you're coming with us!" shouted Geoff as feet thumped up the stairs.

"Teenagers!" he said. "Well today is all about our new arrival. And Janice, I've been thinking about a name. We have to give her a name."

Janice rolled her eyes. "So it's a 'she' is it? And what do you have in mind?"

"How about Lindsay" said Geoff, "after Lindsay Buckingham. You know… you can go your own way, go your own way.." Geoff played his air guitar and thought his cover of the Fleetwood Mac classic was awesome.

"But he's a he!" said Janice. "Although it's one of those ones that can be either I suppose. What about Mac? I like Mac."

Geoff thought a bit. "Mac, hmmm, maybe… I know!" he exclaimed with a beam appearing on his face. "Woody. That's it, Woody. You know, Fleet…Wood, Woody?" He looked at Janice as if he'd just discovered gravity, willing her to agree.

"Woody, yeh I like that, not a she though, but I don't think it really matters these days. Carol in the hairdressers told me there are thirty two genders now, unbelievable!"

Geoff looked at her perplexed.

"Thirty two? Is that why all the toilets are turning unisex? Can't get my head round it. That'll make filling in the next census a nightmare!" He continued trying to think of other things that would take more time but soon lost interest.

"Woody then?"

"Yes, ok, Woody it is!" she proclaimed. And with that they decided to duet the rest of the chorus to the famous (and now infamous) Fleetwood Mac classic. Stevie Nicks and Lindsay Buckingham in full flow.

[Apologies to those non-Fleetwood Mac followers out there. A quick google and you'll quickly get up to speed on this iconic band…and you may need to in order to keep up later on.]

Chapter 13

Geoff looked at his watch, then out of the front window and then at his watch again.

"Sit down man. You've been checking your watch for half an hour. They said 11 o'clock, it's only five to."

"Might be early love," said Geoff. "They said it was a new delivery service so we need to be ready. Hope it's not Uber, they're never on time."

"They won't use Uber to deliver a motorhome you wally!" Janice shook her head and returned to reading her magazine on famous artists. "Hey, did you know Salvador Dali thought he was his own dead brother?"

Geoff turned and stared at Janice in disbelief. "What woman? How does that work?" said Geoff, mildly interested as he liked supernatural stuff.

"Well his older brother died 9 months before he was born and his parents told him he was reincarnated as him. He was called Salvador Dali too! I read it in Now magazine so it must be true!"

Geoff looked puzzled. "Eh? So he was given the same

name as his brother and told he was him? No wonder he painted weird stuff! Hang on! He's here love, he's here!!"

Geoff sprinted to the front door and opened it as their gleaming new Phoenix Crusader III rolled to a halt outside their drive. Mabel, who had been snoozing in her bed, jumped up and figured they were under attack as dad was getting a bit panicky. She side stepped Janice who was on her way to join Geoff and ran to the door barking madly.

"Look" said Geoff. "Its' Stu, the guy who sold us Woody!"

The man who exited the driver's door was indeed Stuart. Mabel recognised him as the tall man with the tasty feet and pushed past Geoff and ran down the drive.

Stuart looked up and froze. "Not again," he thought. "Two days I've been doing this and they send me to all the ones with dogs? Why do they all have dogs?"

Luckily for Stuart, Geoff had kept the gates closed and Mabel was blocked from getting her prize. She prowled up and down along the gates like a tiger assessing her next move.

"Stu! Hello again!" called Geoff. "We'll be right with you. Mabel, inside!"

Mabel turned and looked at dad, looked back to the tall man and headed back inside. "Next time" she thought.

Janice ushered Mabel into the house and shut the door. She joined Geoff at the gates and looked up and down the street to see if anyone had heard their new arrival pull up. Sure enough, Sheila Keane at No 10 was out pruning her roses. Clad in her marigold gloves and short leather skirt, she never missed the opportunity to catch the eye of Mr Carson from No 17, or any other passing eligible "Mr" for that matter.

"Keane by name, keen by nature!" Janice thought but then felt a bit guilty. She did have some sympathy with her as Roger Keane spent a lot of time away from home in his high powered management consulting job.

"He is such a pompous ass," thought Janice. "Always thinks he's better than everyone else, boasting about his sales and client dinners on the expenses. Gives me a leery look every time he passes. Wouldn't surprise me if he's playing away."

Sheila ducked down behind her prize David Austin when she locked eyes with Janice, who smiled and put her arm round Geoff, reassured he knew which side his bread was buttered.

"Well the payment went through ok so I just need you to take a look round and make sure everything is ok, then I'll show you the basics," said Stuart, glancing at the checklist attached to his clipboard.

"No worries" said Geoff. "Leave this to me Janice. I'll handle the technical bits," he winked at Stuart.

Janice rolled her eyes and saw the curtains twitch at No 8 where Julie and Mike Denton never missed a trick.

"Who needs CCTV with neighbours like these?" she thought and smiled to see Geoff excitedly follow Stu around the vehicle.

She began drifting into a world of beautiful scenery with rolling landscapes, lots of shades of green, lakes and sea shores and imagined herself sat painting them in the peace and quiet of nature. Janice longed for her time to paint. People were always surprised when she said she was a painter.

"Ooh really Janice? Didn't know you had it in you,"

they would say. Janice had always been good at art at school but it was only when she'd started painting as a hobby that she got noticed for her talent.

"There's an artist in everyone Janice," Geoff used to say, "Just so happens you're a bloody good one!" She smiled to herself.

At that moment the front door at No 7 opened and Colin and Pat emerged, jostling to get out first.

"Morning Janice!" shouted Pat. "Exciting day!" Colin and Pat were across the road in a flash.

"Wow, this is nice," said Colin. "A beauty. Bet that set you back a bit?"

"Worth every penny!" came a voice from the other side of the motorhome. Geoff carefully steered clear of sharing the £60,000 he had invested in their new 'home from home'. Didn't want the whole street knowing their financial affairs.

"I'm just sorting some technical stuff out with Stu round here. No point explaining it, you need to be in the know with all this." Geoff felt a tad superior that he had the upper-hand with Colin this morning.

"Ah right," shouted Colin "Like how to empty the toilet then?"

"Yes Colin, including that. Life in the outdoors needs specialist knowledge." He tapped the side of his nose as if keeping those secrets to himself.

"Come on Stu, let's get inside. That's where the action is!" Geoff followed Stu through the habitation door.

"You must be dead excited Janice?" said Pat. "When are you going on your first adventure? Bit like a christening isn't it?"

"This Friday," said Janice. "A nice weekend in the Lake District to get used to life in the open air. Lovely campsite, members only. We joined last week and got a 15% discount!" she said smugly and breathed in deeply as if she could already feel the fresh Cumbrian breeze on her face, sitting by Lake Windermere with her brushes and easel.

"Hope it's got facilities," said Colin. "You don't want Geoff christening the pot do you?"

"Colin!" shouted Pat and dug him in the ribs. "It's outdoor living. What do you think they did before Armitage Shanks?"

"Oh yes, it's got five star facilities, even got Dyson hairdryers!" retorted Janice. "We can live the life of Riley or not, that's the beauty of motorhoming - choices, choices…!"

Everyone then tried to put the image of Geoff on the loo out of their mind.

"Anyway, I think Gail is coming with us," said Janice, quickly changing the subject. "She's at that funny age. Thinks she's an adult but isn't. I'm not having her home alone if she hits it off with that Chesney. When I was her age…"

"Oh our Robbie knows him. Bit of a lady's man from what I hear," said Pat. "You want to watch that one!"

"Exactly!" said Janice and folded her arms as if preparing for combat.

Geoff emerged from Woody beaming. "Well that's all done, pretty straightforward really." Stu followed him a little nervously.

"Yes, erm Mr Watt seems very confident he knows what to do," he said. "Although I should really have shown you the full LED panel features and shown you how to change the gas cylinders over…" Stu frantically looked down his checklist, realising there were a few boxes still to be ticked before the customer declaration bit where Geoff was to sign.

"Ah you're alright," said Geoff waving his hands in the air. " It's all in the manual! How hard can it all be?"

Janice sighed and rolled her eyes. "Here we go" she said. "Living the dream with Frank Spencer!" *[Google that name if you're under 45 years old or don't watch UK Gold].*

"Ay, did they find out who caused that flood at the motorhome show?" Colin asked Stu eagerly. "I can't wait to find out what happened!"

"All I heard was they were studying the CCTV but there wasn't a camera where the Gladiator 1000 was. Don't know why as it's the most expensive one in the show. £15,000 damage apparently so someone will be keeping their head down!" Stu shook his head vigorously.

Janice glanced knowingly at Geoff who quickly changed the subject.

"Well, we've got some packing to do Janice, can't hang around here chatting all day! Thanks Stu, where do I sign?"

And with that, Geoff signed the delivery and inspection note and Stu handed over an extremely thick user manual.

"Happy reading!" said Stu and away he went to unclip a strange looking electric bike from the cycle rack attached to the back of Woody. He took a helmet from a pillion box on the back and prepared himself for departure.

"I'll just go get that magazine you wanted to borrow," said Janice to Pat and, as she opened the gate, Gail opened the front door. In the blink of an eye, Mabel saw her chance and raced out of the front door, down the drive and out of the gate towards Stu, barking madly.

"Arrrgh!" shouted Stu.

"Mabel!" shouted Janice and Geoff together.

Stu managed to turn on the little engine on the bike and started to move off just as Mabel reached his right leg.

"That's the one that had that red stuff on I'm sure," Mabel thought.

Stu revved the throttle more and more and slowly began to speed up with Mabel running at his side down Sycamore Avenue.

"Help!" he shouted.

Mabel just managed to grab his trouser leg at the bottom, tugging it just enough to make Stu veer off the road towards No 10.

By this time Geoff and Janice had begun pursuit down the road shouting Mabel to come back, threatening to return her to the Dogs Trust – something that never seemed to worry her when Mabel was on a mission.

"Help! Call it off!" Stu shouted with Mabel hanging on for dear life. He found himself heading straight for the garden wall of No 10 in front of where Sheila Keane was still pruning the same rose bush.

"Oh no!" shouted Geoff.

"Heavens!" shouted Janice.

"Mummy!" shouted Stu.

Mabel realised this was not going well and decided to let go just as the front wheel hit the wall. The momentum sent the back end of the bike upwards catapulting Stu, who's eyes were now tightly shut, up and over the small wall into the garden where he landed flat on his back at the feet of Mrs Keane.

"Oooooh!" said Sheila, "I've had a few men fall for me but never like this!"

And with that she bent down over Stu to see if there was any damage, revealing just enough of her ample bosom.

"Are you a stunt man?"

A little dazed, Stu opened his eyes and came face to face with Sheila's cleavage, carefully crafted between her push up bra and low cut top.

"Oh my!" he cried "Have I died and gone to heaven?"

"Well, almost my little stunt king. Let me get you inside and I'll check you over for any injuries. Don't worry, I used to be a nurse you know, so I've seen it all before."

And with that, she helped the groggy motorhome salesman to his feet, put her arm around him and shepherded him through the front door.

"There, there," she said, her hand getting lower and lower until it rested on his bottom.

"Now let's get these trousers off…" and the door slammed shut.

"Another victim," said Geoff as he and Janice reached the drive at No 10. "Poor Stu. She'll eat him alive!"

"Mabel, come here you naughty girl!" Janice shouted. "Whatever were you doing chasing him like that. Come on Geoff, everybody's looking!"

They marched Mabel back up the street to No 7 where Gail was talking to Colin and Pat.

"Wow, this is cool!" she said pointing at Woody. "Can I bring a friend with me when we go away?"

"Not this time love," said Janice. We need to get used to it, or at least your dad does! Maybe another time."

Gail's face dropped. "A weekend with the parents, great!" she thought.

"See you later Pat, we'll get that cuppa when we get back. Come on Mabel, inside." And with that, Janice frogmarched the disappointed Cocker into the house.

"Is Robbie in?" asked Gail. "Thought I might go down to the park and he could bring his skateboard."

"Yes he is love," said Pat and Gail trotted up the path of No 5 to prise her friend away from his Xbox.

"Are you sure you know what you need to know Geoff?" said Colin pointing to the user manual tucked under Geoff's arm. "That looks mighty thick to me."

"They don't call me the motorhome wizard for nothing!" said Geoff tapping the side of his nose. "Anyway, must get on. I've this beauty to get ready for our first adventure."

"Well, good luck," said Colin. "You're gonna need it!"

"Colin!" said Pat poking him in the ribs. "You're only jealous because you're putting up those shelves this weekend. Don't listen to him Geoff. You'll have a lovely time and looks like the weather's going to hold up." And with that they all gazed up to the sky watching the sun peek out between the broken clouds.

"Oh yes!" exclaimed Geoff. "I booked that in nice and early too! See you later." And he turned and disappeared through the habitation door to inspect his precious new baby.

[note to readers: don't be a Geoff and rely on the manual, you'll see why later. And for those who didn't

watch television in the 1970s, Frank was a calamitous, well intended, character who's projects always ended in disaster. There really isn't an equivalent these days, except Geoff maybe...]

Chapter 14

"Today's the day Janice!" shouted Geoff as he put a cup of tea on the side table next to their bed. "In a few hours we'll be out in nature in all its glory."

"It's seven o'clock!" exclaimed Janice. "We can't check in until 1pm! We packed everything last night!"

"Ah but preparation is everything," said Geoff firmly. "Fail to prepare, prepare to fail as…well, someone said. I need to double check the list you laminated for me. And we need to get Gail out of bed. That'll take until midday!"

Geoff had already fed Mabel who was sat in her bed in the kitchen watching Geoff read his list and mightily curious about the activities mum and dad were doing yesterday. She was very concerned they were preparing to bring a new dog into the family to live in the big van that was now parked on the drive. Mum had put a new dog bed, bowls and toys in there and she could have sworn she saw some of her favourite treats in her hand at one point.

"Why do they need another dog when they have me?" She thought.

Geoff read through his list.

"Food, drinks, clothes, bedding, toiletries, medication, coats, walking boots, other shoes, hey who has added all these shoes?! Unbelievable! Anyway, what's next… washing stuff, technology…good grief, iPad, iPhones, firestick, kindles, I thought we were getting away from all this madness!!"

"You'll be complaining if you haven't got your kindle to read on a night man," said Janice as she entered the kitchen.

"And we need the iPad for that app that shows us how to get there. Gail won't come if we don't have Wi-Fi, have you sorted that?"

Geoff sighed. "I think so. I got one of those miffy things with a sim card. Tried it last night and seems to work ok. Anyway, it's a chance to get her off all that technology. I've put her bike on the back so she can get some proper exercise in the fresh air!"

"I heard that!" shouted a voice from upstairs. "I need my phone in case Chesney needs me."

Geoff sighed again. "That Mr bloody one and only!" he whispered under his breath.

Janice had also laminated a sheet for what Geoff called technical checks. He peered at it moving the sheet to and from his face.

"Why don't you put your glasses on love? That's what they're for!" enquired Janice.

"Can't remember where I put them," replied Geoff.

"Here," said Janice. "They were on the coffee table where you left them!"

Geoff looked at the technical list.

"Right then – tyre pressure, oil, water, gas bottles, all

windows closed, all stuff secured down, no shake, rattle and roll love!" he exclaimed and began a sit down jive.

"We don't want Bill Haley in the house!"

"I'll check all the cupboards as I need to make sure we've got everything," said Janice, ignoring his rock 'n' roll revival.

"Good love, always important to have someone in charge of something," replied Geoff, feeling ever so slightly in charge of proceedings.

"Toilet cassette to prepare, fresh and waste water tanks and taps to check. Easy!" he declared. "Well, if you're an expert that is."

"We'll see," said Janice. "They say you always forget something!"

During the next couple of hours Geoff checked, rechecked and checked the rechecking of his lists and decided at last they were ready.

"Gail, we're going!" he shouted and looked over at Mabel.

"What's been the matter with you all morning? Sat there sulking for some reason." He looked at Janice as she checked her handbag for the fifth time.

"I dunno. Maybe she thinks we're leaving her here," she said. "Come on Mabel, we're going on holibobs!"

Mabel suddenly sat up and realised all the goodies in the new thing were for her. She jumped out of her bed and ran to the front door, wagging her tail franticly.

"There you go," said Janice "she's happy now!"

"Gail!!" Janice's voice carried much further than Geoff's.

"I'm coming," replied Gail. "Caitlin is in crisis and I'm her mental guru."

"God help her!" said Geoff and with that he opened the front door and he, Janice and Mabel headed out to Woody, who was sat ready and waiting on the drive.

Five minutes later, Gail emerged from the front door and then ran back in and re-emerged two minutes later with her phone glued to her ear.

A minute later she was clicking in her seatbelt at the table seat behind the front driver's cab (facing front). She still had her phone to her ear.

"No Caitlin, that's exactly what he'll expect you to do so you need to do the opposite. Don't let him think he knows the rules!"

Janice smiled. "That's my girl," she said and tapped Geoff on his knee. "Keep 'em on their toes, eh Geoff?"

"My toes are worn to the bone woman," he said and chuckled.

Mabel felt very important as she settled on her new bed between the two front seats. Her sibling rivalry with Gail was continuous and knowing she was further to the front was a point scored today. She looked up at mum and dad and was very excited that it was Gail and not her that was relegated to the back this time.

"She needs her seat belt on," said Geoff. Janice turned and saw an extension lead attached to the seat belt on the chair opposite Gail. She leaned over and attached it to Mabel's collar, giving her a chance to get in some face licks.

"Urrrghhh!" shouted Janice. "Gerroff Mabel. What did she have for breakfast?"

"Chicken and Kangaroo," laughed Geoff. "No wonder she's bouncing around. Get it? Bouncing around?"

Janice sighed and rolled her eyes. "Yes man, I get it! Now let's get going!"

Geoff turned the key and the engine purred into life. He turned to Janice.

"This is it babe, now we're motoring!" And with that he started to reverse out of the drive.

"Don't you think I should direct you as this is your first time driving it?" said Janice "I don't think you can see…"

He'd gone about five feet when a horn blared behind them and he slammed on the brakes. Geoff wound down the window and looked behind only to see Colin doing the same from the front seat of his car.

"Morning campers!" shouted Colin. "Nearly a bit of déjà vu there!"

"You muppet!" shouted Geoff. "You'd have known about it if you'd hit my Woody!"

"Woody is it?" shouted Colin. "As in Woody Woodpecker?" and did some strange high-pitched laugh that sounded like he'd swallowed a bottle of helium.

"I told you," said Janice and got out of the passenger door.

"What are you two like!" she shouted to Colin and waved him on before navigating Geoff and Woody out of the drive. Safely pointing the right way, Janice jumped back into her seat and buckled up.

"Right then. Ready Gail? Ready Mabel?" Gail was lost in her headphones and Mabel gave a wag of her tail. "Right babe, let's do this!"

And with that they set off on their first adventure…

[Note to readers: Motorhoming isn't just about where you get to, it's about the journey there…]

Chapter 15

"Watch the wing mirrors!!" shouted Janice as Geoff navigated the small roads that led to the A65 along their route to the Lake District.

"No sweat!" replied Geoff. "35 years driving and never lost a wing mirror yet," he boasted.

"Well you weren't driving one of these all that time were you?" Janice countered. "When we hired that one in Scotland from Gordon, all he went on about was the box of wing mirrors he had in his garage! Cost a fortune to replace he said."

"Stop fretting woman. You're distracting me!"

Soon they were out of Beddlesford and on the A road towards Skipton.

"Look Janice. Less than half an hour and we're in the heart of the dales already. This is the tip of the iceberg!"

"As long as we're not on the Titanic!" she blasted.

Geoff did one of his soulful sighs. He looked out over the rolling green hills and felt a sudden reassurance things were going to be ok.

"Nature has a way of doing that," he thought and

turned on the radio to hear strains of Born to Be Wild by Steppenwolf.

"Would you listen to that babe? That's us that is!"

"Yes dear," replied Janice and returned to her Closer magazine where she was getting the low down on Jonny Depp's latest misdemeanour.

Geoff glanced back and saw Gail deep in conversation with, well, it could be anyone and then looked down at Mabel who was fast asleep, probably warmed by the air blowing from the vents in front of her. Geoff felt happy, this was what he had dreamed of all those years.

While he worked his socks off for other people, he always wanted to live life on his terms and do the things he really enjoyed. At times work had been a slog, like it is for most people. He had done well and been paid well. He could remember lots of rewarding times, but also much of it being doing stuff 'because someone said so.'

"How much time do we waste on meaningless stuff," he thought.

With age, he'd realised how much work had dominated his life. Now he was determined to reverse that.

"Whatever I do next will be on my terms," he said to himself. "That's what he liked about Janice's business. She earned from it but mostly she loved what she did and that would last a lifetime."

Geoff recalled the words of a colleague when he had begun rethinking his future. "Work out how much is enough Geoff, rather than how much you can get."

"Wise words," thought Geoff and manoeuvred Woody around the next major roundabout onto the M6 North.

A few miles further on Geoff waved frantically out of the window shouting "Alright mate!"

"What on earth are you doing?" exclaimed Janice. "Did you know them?"

"No babe. It's what motorhomers do. We always give each other a little wave. Not caravaners though, they aren't in the club and anyway, they're spending too much time making sure their rear end isn't rockin 'n' rolling!"

Janice laughed. "Oooh look there's another!" And they both waved frantically at the motorhome heading past them on the other side of the motorway.

"This is the life!" exclaimed Geoff.

A few miles further on, Mabel stood up and tried to jump onto Janice's knee. She got about half way up when the seat belt lead pulled taught and she dropped back down.

"Mabel, watch it!" shouted Geoff.

"I think she needs a wee," said Janice. "We've been going a while now."

"Ok," said Geoff . "We'll pull into the next services. I saw a sign back there and it's only a couple of miles away."

Sure enough, Geoff turned Woody into the next service station and followed the signs to the lorry park.

"Why do they not have proper parking for us motorhomers?" Geoff complained. "There are thousands of us now and they don't even designate a spot."

"Maybe they think we'll camp overnight?" said Janice "Not that I'd want to, what with all these lorry drivers about. Do you remember that documentary we watched with that lorry driver serial killer? Makes me feel a bit edgy being in here surrounded by them."

"No, that wasn't a lorry driver, he was a taxi driver," countered Geoff.

"Don't you remember? He was known as the Taxidermist cos he stuffed his victims and put them in his own version of Madam Tussauds. What a weirdo!"

Janice thought hard and then remembered with a sigh of relief.

"Ah ok, well that's ok then – pull in here. Do you want me to navigate you in?"

"Oi, cheeky mare! I could park this with my eyes closed," said Geoff as he manoeuvred Woody into the bay between two huge articulated lorries.

"Are we here?" came a voice from behind, "This place is a bit of a dump. I'm hungry."

Gail had returned to the land of the living and looked up from her iPad just as Woody came to a stop.

"No," said Janice, "Mabel needs a wee so we've stopped for a break. May as well have some lunch now we're here."

"Oh yeh, I feel peckish now you've said that babe," said Geoff.

"I need the toilet too," said Gail.

"Well it's just No. 1s in Woody," said Geoff. "No. 2s are banned!"

"Dad!" Gail shouted and made her way inside the bathroom.

"And don't forget to open the hatch!"

[Note to readers: for the uneducated, using a motorhome toilet takes a bit of getting used to, especially when it comes to the hatch, and there are many theories on whether the hatch should be open or closed at the point of well, impact, if you get my meaning. To give you an idea, just remember

'open hatch – do the thing – press the flush – wait a few seconds – close the hatch. There, now you know.]

"I'll take Mabel for a quick walk while you put the kettle on babe," said Geoff and Mabel's head swivelled round when she heard the W word.

"That's the beauty of having your own home from home," he grinned.

Geoff unclipped Mabel's seat belt and replaced it with her 'walkies' lead, sending Mabel into a frenzy. She dragged Geoff to the habitation door and whimpered, she really did need to go.

"She really does need to go," said Geoff and opened the door.

"See you soon, watch for traffic. I'll make some sandwiches too. Cheese and pickle on its way."

For the first time in her adult life, Janice found herself wondering how to make a cup of tea. That sounds odd but Geoff had mentioned not everything worked when there was no mains hook up, but anyway it was always important to turn on the power on the control panel above the door. She remembered that bit.

Janice reached up and pressed the power button. The LED display lit up and showed the fridge was ok and the lights were ok, not that they needed lights in the middle of the day. But there was a big triangle with an exclamation mark in it for the water pump. She pressed the button and heard a high pitched beep followed by the panel showing *ERR 483*.

"Don't understand that," she thought. "Right, I'll just turn on the tap."

Janice turned on the tap and nothing happened.

"What the…! Where's the water? Gail, fetch me one of those bottles of still water from under your seat. I don't think your dad has put any water in the tank. Good grief man, lucky I put in some bottles!"

Gail reached in for the emergency supply and Janice filled the kettle. She plugged in their new DeLonghi kettle she had colour matched with the little cushions she had carefully selected and flicked the switch. Nothing.

"What now?! Doesn't anything work in here?" she barked. "Gail, pass me the whistling kettle from under the other seat."

"A whistling kettle? What the heck?" Gail reached in and lifted out one of those old fashioned kettles that you put on the hob. "How does it whistle then?" she said looking under the base for where you put the batteries.

"When the water boils, it whistles to tell you it's ready." Janice explained. "Your grandma used one right up until she went into the home. She never trusted electricity, thought it was a fire hazard. Mind you, so was she. I remember when she fell asleep and left it whistling until it ran dry. Lucky the noise drove her cat so mad it leapt on her to wake her up. It was only a small fire the fireman said but god bless that cat! It must have been its ninth life cos it got run over the following week - by a fire engine of all things!"

Gail shook her head in disbelief. "You couldn't make it up in this family," she exclaimed.

Janice filled the whistling kettle and put it on the stove, crossing her fingers in her head, she turned on the hob and pressed the ignition. Sure enough, that reassuring sound of a flame met her ears and she gave a sigh of relief.

"We have heat! Right Gail, put that phone down and butter this bread."

"Awww mum, Naomi can't decide which lipstick to wear when she meets Jed tonight and she's halfway through putting on *Ravenous Rouge*, which is so millennial. I always advise her on what looks best!"

"Well your dad will be ravenous when he gets back so tell Naomi you'll sort her lippy after lunch. Come on, this is outdoor living, everyone mucks in."

"Sorry chuck, have to go, be back in a bit. Don't choose without me. You remember what happened with Luke, he freaked at the *Morticia Mauve*. Laters hun!"

When Geoff returned with Mabel, he found Janice outside Woody where she had set up their three folding chairs and the fold out table on which she was flattening out her new M&S waterproof tablecloth.

"Good grief Janice," exclaimed Geoff. "You look like you're here for the week!"

"Well, I thought it would be nice to sit out now the sun's come out. Everything's ready. Gail! Get off that phone and come and have your lunch."

"There was no water in the tap. Did you put any in the tank?" Janice asked.

"No babe, keeping the payload down until we get there. Forgot to tell you but Mabel was desperate. This looks great though. Ay, pass me a sausage roll."

So there they were, the three of them sat down for their first outdoor lunch with Woody, in the middle of a lorry park services just off the M6. And they were loving it! As each lorry driver drove past they gave a little wave and Geoff raised his new *Dad's Motorhome* mug to say hello.

"Beats paying a fortune in there," said Geoff pointing to the building housing all the eating places and shops. "They rip you off 'cos they know you're in the middle of nowhere. Not us though!"

"You're not wrong babe," said Janice as she sipped her hot tea from her bone china cup. "You're not wrong. No one tops my cheese and pickle sarnies!"

Chapter 16

Around forty five minutes later, they were packed up and back on the road.

Geoff turned on the radio to the sounds of *[guess who]* – Fleetwood Mac.

"Hey love, listen to that! It's like Woody knows what to play! Ooooh, I wanna be with you everywhere…ahhhh oooohhhh…"

Janice joined in and they were in heaven, on their way to freedom singing their hearts out. Gail looked up as she saw her mum pretending to hold a microphone, waving her head from side to side.

She pulled her headphones to one side for a few seconds, rolled her eyes and smiled inwardly, happy to see her mum and dad living their dream.

After waving to several more motorhomers on the next stage of the journey, Geoff steered Woody towards their first campsite.

Lakeside View Touring Park had some great reviews, except for one warden who was labelled "a bit of a jobsworth".

Soon they were greeted by a welcome sign promising tranquillity and the best facilities in the Lake District.

"Here we are babe! Oooh, it looks nice," exclaimed Geoff.

Ahead of them was a landscaped entrance with a large wooden lodge hosting a "Reception" sign above the door. Beyond they could see nice spacious pitches, all hardstanding *[that's covered in small stone])* with a small patch of plush green grass to the side.

Geoff pulled into the bay for new arrivals and unbuckled his seatbelt. Mabel, sensing it was time for another walk leapt towards him only to be garrotted by her own seatbelt.

"You daft dog!" Janice shouted. "Let daddy go and check us in, then you can have a nice walk."

Geoff entered the reception and walked up to the counter. He was greeted by a grey haired chap with small glasses dressed in what Geoff thought must be their uniform – it reminded Geoff of when he was in the boy scouts and thought the man was just missing his woggle to have the complete kit. His name badge said Roger.

"Good afternoon Mr…" enquired Roger.

"Watt" Geoff replied.

"Your name? Mr…?" Roger enquired again.

"Watt, it's Geoff Watt," Geoff sighed, "here with the wife and young 'un for a couple of nights."

"Ah yes, here we go Mr Watt. Two nights on a standard pitch, just electric, no water. We've reserved No. 13 for you, unlucky for some!"

Roger chuckled to himself and Geoff felt a little uneasy.

"It says here two adults, one child and a dog. We need

to know exact, you see. I once had a chap who paid for one adult and he had a wife and 4 children in his VW campervan. God knows how they all fit in along with the two greyhounds!" exclaimed Roger, looking Geoff up and down for signs of doubt.

"Yep, that's the clan," Geoff replied, trying to loosen up.

"Tried losing the daughter at the service station but she kept finding us!"

Geoff sniggered but Roger didn't seem to get the joke and just stared at him down his spectacles.

"Why? Is she badly behaved?" asked Roger. "We have high standards at Lakeside View, five star reviews you know. Except for that fool who…, well never mind that."

"Errr, no. She's a diamond, just a bit rough around the edges!" said Geoff and then felt a bit awkward that he'd stoke the fire again.

"And the dog, is he well behaved? Must be on a lead at all times."

Roger leaned over to collect a piece of paper that had spurted out of the printer next to him.

"There's plenty of bins around the site, we don't like mess on this site. Five stars for cleanliness at Lakeside View."

"No, errr, yes," spluttered Geoff. "It's a she and she's…" he decided it wasn't worth it and took the sheet from Roger.

"That's your receipt. Here's a map of the site and where all the facilities are. Best facilities in the Lakes these are. Five star, we keep 'em clean and the guests keep 'em clean. If you get my meaning?" Roger look tellingly at Geoff.

"I do," agreed Geoff, wondering if they had arrived at a campsite or a bootcamp.

"We're all very clean…" he mumbled and then regretted it straight away.

"Well, any problems and I'm here every day. I'm Roger," said Roger and pointed to his name badge. "I'm well known around here."

"I'll bet you are," thought Geoff and headed back to Woody to re-join his clean, well behaved family.

"Well?" Janice enquired. "All sorted?"

"Well and truly. I feel like I've just been interrogated by the campsite gestapo! Let's hope that's the last we've seen of him!"

Chapter 17

Geoff steered Woody around the campsite until they reached pitch 13. He drove forwards onto the pitch and rolled down his window to check his positioning.

"You have to reverse in," said a voice to his right. "Otherwise you'll have the wrath of Roger to deal with!"

Geoff saw the voice was coming from a man sat in his camping chair in front of his motorhome on the next pitch.

"Thanks mate," said Geoff. "I'm still recovering from the check-in! Janice, can you guide me in?"

After what must have been a thirty five point turn, Woody was set facing the right way and Geoff breathed a sigh of relief.

"Let me just check the levelling," he said. "We don't want everything rolling to one end like it did when we pitched that tent at that campsite at Surprising View. Couldn't fault the view but I never did find that tin of beans…"

He opened his phone and clicked on his new 'spirit level' app.

"Right Gail, put that on the table and see what it says." Geoff handed the phone to his daughter and she did as instructed.

"Looks like we're sloping towards the front dad," she said peering at the little bubble on the screen.

"Ok, I can sort that out easy enough," said Geoff, looking from Gail to Janice and tapping the side of his nose.

Geoff produced a bag from the back of the driver's seat and pulled out two big yellow plastic triangle-shaped things.

"Chocks" he said proudly, "for under the wheels! Janice, can you put them at the front wheels and I'll drive up them to level us off."

Janice felt a bit nervous about her husband driving a three and a half tonne vehicle towards her but bit her lip, took the chocks and disappeared in front of the bonnet, carefully placing them in front of the wheels.

She gave the thumbs up to Geoff who had now got back into the driving seat and started up the engine. He edged Woody forwards as Janice beckoned him on like one of those aircraft people with the table tennis bats.

"Bit more" she said, "a bit further…" she said, waving her arms at him.

Geoff pressed the clutch and accelerator carefully to edge further up the chocks. At the same time, Mabel got to her feet and realised mum had unbuckled her lead. She was so excited she leapt up onto Geoff's lap causing him to lose control of his feet. In an instant Woody leapt forward, up and over the top of the chocks and landed back on the floor with a thud.

"Stop you madman!!" shouted Janice diving out of the way.

Geoff slammed hard on the brakes and stopped Woody instantly, but he couldn't see where Janice had gone after her Gordon Banks like dive to her right. The memory of his driving test emergency stop flashed before him and briefly he felt a tinge of pride that he'd passed that test again. That was suddenly replaced by the fact he may have just run over his wife.

"Mabel, get down!" he shouted. "Gail, take the dog, I think I've run over your mother."

Geoff leapt out and rushed to the front of Woody. Janice was lying on the floor with most of her body outside the line of Woody's front wheels. Her instinctive dive had left only her legs in the way and Geoff saw the front wheel had stopped about a foot from her legs.

By now the chap next door, who had been monitoring Geoff's manoeuvring capability, had come across to see what damage was done.

"Have you squashed her?" he enquired, peering from a few feet away.

"No he hasn't!" came a shrill from Janice. "But I'll bloody squash him when I get up! What the hell...?"

"It was Mabel love, you let her off the lead and she went mad!"

"Oh so it's might fault you nearly killed me! Help me up you stupid man."

Gail came out of the habitation door with Mabel on her extendable lead. Seeing mum on the ground, she saw an opportunity for kisses and jumped on her licking her face wildly.

"Urrghh, alright Mabel. I know it wasn't your fault. Daddy's an idiot and thinks he knows how to drive but he doesn't. If he's not reversing into neighbours' cars he's trying to run me over."

"That was five years ago woman and it was Colin's fault! Anyway, up you get," he said, pulling her to her feet and dusting her down.

"Look no harm done. Let me get this sorted and the hook up in and we'll have a cuppa. Gail, get the tea stuff out for your mother."

"I can help you get on the chocks," said their neighbour. "My name's Brian and I'm guessing this is your first time?"

"Well, sort of but I know what I'm doing mate, just a technical difficulty caused by a mad cocker spaniel! Maybe a quick steer would help though."

Brian helped Geoff steer Woody onto the chocks and Gail confirmed the level was much better, albeit she could still get her stress ball to roll forward a bit when she tried, claiming her test was better than the app.

Geoff plugged in the hook up *[beginners note: Woody first not the mains - to avoid risk of electric shock]* and shouted Janice that she could put the kettle on.

Brian had returned to his seat but had kept an eye on Geoff's routine.

"I remember our first trip back in '97," shouted Brian.

"Bev, that's my wife and me, well we made everything up as we went along. We parked on the wrong pitch and then forgot to fill up the water before I pitched up and…"

"Oh eck! Janice, hang on…"

"Geoff, there's no water! What's going on?!"

Geoff poked his head inside and confessed he'd forgot

it was a standard pitch and not fully serviced *[yep that one has a water tap]* so he'd have to drive round and fill up the tank.

"Can you put the Wi-Fi on first dad? There's a campsite one but its rubbish!" complained Gail.

"No you can wait 'til we're all set up Gail. Surely your friends can wait a bit!"

"Well if I don't sort Naomi's lipstick soon, she's gonna make the biggest mistake of her life…"

"Good grief," Geoff sighed as he went to unplug the hook up. "Just a few more minutes and I can relax…"

Chapter 18

Half an hour later, the tank was full. With Janice refusing to go anywhere near the front of Woody with Geoff at the wheel, Brian had once again steered Geoff onto the chocks. The hook up was plugged in, the table and chairs were out and Gail was happy inside as the Wi-Fi miffy thing fed her iPhone with her social calendar.

Janice was sat out on their camp chairs [*five star rated on Amazon but snapped up cheaper with a discount card at Go Camp*] with her steaming cup of tea and a copy of Closer magazine. Mabel was lying contentedly at her feet, occasionally licking her toes that protruded out of her flipflops. Geoff joined her with a can of beer. He sat down, clicked open the can and took a long hard swig.

"Ahhh, that's better babe. This is the life, now we can relax. Bit of a bumpy start but it's all part of the adventure!"

"Bit of a bumpy start? What, running over your wife? Part of the adventure? Anyway, I've told my mother if anything happens to me, you're the prime suspect. She said you would be anyway, even if you were in another country."

"Nice" said Geoff. "I do love your mother, good old Maureen," said Geoff thoughtfully, remembering their wedding day and when Maureen pinned him against the vestry wall and said she would track him down like a dog if he didn't treat her Janice properly. "You always know where you stand with Mo."

"You know she doesn't like it when you call her that," said Janice.

Geoff gave a little smile and took another sip of his chilled lager.

"Well if Colin and Pat could see us now. Fresh air, peace and quiet. That sun is just right, no need for cream on today. Hey look over there, they look like they've come to party."

Janice looked to where Geoff was nodding his head in an awkward 'so they can't see me' fashion. She spotted a row of three motorhomes lined up on grass pitches opposite. Six people were sat at the table of the middle one, laughing and joking merrily as they handed round drinks and snacks.

"They must all be in their sixties," said Janice. "Aw, well that's lovely. That'll be us in a few year's Geoff."

"Well I hope that bowl in the middle of the table isn't for their motorhome keys. I read somewhere there's a few swingers in the camping game you know."

"They're just having a good time Geoff. You've a mind like a sewer."

Geoff looked around a bit further and saw all the pitches were full. With Brian on one side on pitch 15, he spotted another couple with a caravan sat out on pitch 11. They were a little younger than themselves with a lad whom he presumed was their son and must be a similar age to Gail. He was dressed all in black and had a gothic look about him. Geoff waved as the couple looked up and they waved back.

"What's our plan then babe?" he said to Janice. "I thought we could have that lasagne you cooked tonight and then I'll do a BBQ tomorrow night. The weather's looking good and I want to test out the new kit."

"Always food first with you isn't it man? Well let me relax a bit and then I'll put the oven on. I want to do a bit of sketching if the weather's good tomorrow so I can take it back to paint over. Why don't you take Mabel for a walk with Gail after tea – get her out in some fresh air and off that phone!"

"Ok, good idea. We can walk down by the lake," he said, as he took another swig of his beer and glanced through the campsite leaflet Roger had given him. A photo showed a serene view of the lake with a man paddle-boarding and a couple walking there dog along the path that circled the vast bowl of water. "Looks nice and relaxing here babe. Got a good feeling about this trip."

Geoff and Janice settled into their chairs and started to feel the freedom they had hoped for when they conceived their motorhome dream.

Chapter 19

The Watts enjoyed their lasagne as the evening sun began to cool.

Janice was very pleased with her table arrangements but scowled as Geoff squirted tomato sauce onto her new table cloth as well as his plate.

"Lucky it's Geoff proof!" she exclaimed as she wiped the mess up.

She looked around at the neighbouring pitches and saw a variety of groups, mainly families and couples enjoying the fresh air and al fresco dining. A dad was playing Swing ball with his son, another was setting up a BBQ while his Labrador eyed up the fresh sausages on the table next to him.

Across the way, a couple were sat relaxing with a glass of Rosé while their daughter sat and coloured in a book. She knew now why getting away was so important and it reminded her why she loved painting so much. Getting close to nature made you feel good, simple as that.

Watching Gail tuck into her lasagne and garlic bread, she hoped her daughter would come to appreciate the goodness of her natural surroundings.

"Gail, your dad wants to explore the lakeside and so I want you to keep an eye on him. Take Mabel with you while I wash up and then I want to see what the facilities are like. I brought us that new conditioner so we'll go get showers later."

Janice loved the outdoors but also loved her creature comforts. She was passed the days of washing your face in a stream outside your tent and now much preferred the hot showers and electric hairdryers promised on the campsite websites she'd been scouring over the last few months.

"Yeh, ok but I want to get back for the latest Divine Diva podcast – she's got 10 ways to get your guy this week."

Geoff rolled his eyes. "Good grief, is this to go after that Chesney again?"

"No dad, he's old news! It's Damian in my Geography class now. Gemma Stevens is after him now he's single and I can't let her win."

"I can't keep up girl. Well leave your phone here and give your hormones a rest!"

A few minutes later, Geoff and Gail were headed down to the lake with Mabel pulling ahead on her lead for all she was worth.

"Slow down Mabel! Good grief dog, you'll strangle yourself at this rate!" shouted Geoff but it made not one jot of difference to Mabel who loved nothing better than to paddle in water at every opportunity.

"It's nice and peaceful here dad," said Gail as they stood at the water's edge. "I wonder how deep this lake is in the middle?"

"Let's not find out eh?" said Geoff recalling his wet experience at the motorhome show. A tingle went down his spine at the thought and he could have sworn he felt a trickle of water follow shortly behind.

As they walked around the lake, they saw a man fishing at one of several small wooden piers that were positioned a few yards around the water.

As they approached the fisherman, Geoff could see he was all kitted out with the latest gear and dressed for the occasion. He wore a green jacket covered in pockets of all shapes and sizes and long waders with what looked like braces over his shoulders to keep them in place. On his head was a tweed trilby with a few furry brightly coloured hooks dotted around the rim.

"Caught much?" said Geoff

"Nope" said the man, fairly disinterested with his audience. He eyed Mabel as she tried to pull Geoff towards his maggot box. Mabel thought the wriggling little worms looked very appetising, if a little small.

"We've just arrived today, not much of a fisherman myself. Is it easy?"

"Nope" said the man again as he threaded something like a lead weight onto the fishing line on the end of his rod.

"Well, good luck!" said Geoff thinking he wasn't going to get much more conversation out of this chap.

"Don't need luck," said the fisherman. "Just peace and quiet".

Geoff looked at Gail and raised his eyebrows. They both tiptoed away from the lakeside, Geoff pulling Mabel just as she spotted a piece of bread next to the maggot box.

"Come on Mabel, leave the nice man to catch his fish."

They walked further round the lake, taking in the greenery and watching the various birds as they circled over the water and occasionally dived head first into the lake. One eventually emerged with a small fish in its beak and was quickly harassed by the others who had not been so successful. Geoff breathed in deeply and felt good, this was what it was all about, getting back to nature and blending in.

"So how's school then?" asked Geoff.

"It's ok," said Gail. "I'll be glad when my mocks are out of the way." Gail was in the middle of revising for her GCSEs and finding it a struggle to balance all her studies with her busy social life.

"Well when I took my exams, they were O'levels in our day. I remember Wimbledon being on while I was revising and your gran took my tv out of my bedroom to stop me watching. You didn't have catch up tv back then so you had to wait until the highlights came on and that was after 10 o'clock so I missed most of it that year!"

"I don't like tennis dad," said Gail giving him a look only a sixteen year old can give.

"That's not the point, although it would be if it was match-point," chuckled Geoff to himself.

"I have no idea what you're on about dad," groaned Gail.

"What I mean is you have to make sacrifices in the short term to get where you need to be for the long term. By putting the effort in now, you'll be glad later."

"Yes, I know, it's just so difficult when everyone seems to be doing stuff while I'm revising." Gail moaned.

"Well yes I get that. Hey, why don't we get the swing ball out later and I'll give you a good whipping!"

"What like the last time when I beat you three to nil? Ha ha, ok, you're on!"

Geoff was glad he'd given Gail something to smile about. He remembered vaguely being her age and knew now it was even harder with social media and all the pressures that brings, especially for girls. All he could do was his best as a dad and give her a chance to find out things herself, eventually!

They walked a bit further and then turned back after Mabel had completed her round of toilet stops. Gail dropped a pretty full pooh bag into one of the many bins scattered around the park, pulling a scrunched up face and cursing whatever Mabel had eaten last.

As they returned the way they had come, they approached the fisherman they'd seen earlier. Suddenly, they saw him spring to his feet, jerking his rod and watched as the rod bent like a piece of bamboo. As he stood, he knocked his chair over and started shouting.

"I think it's the one, yes I think this is it. They always said there was a 20 pounder in here but no one has ever landed it!"

He stumbled towards his landing net *[that's the one that scoops up the fish]* but couldn't quite reach it while he concentrated on not losing the fish.

"Hey mate, that looks massive," shouted Geoff. "Need a hand?"

"Grab that net for me!" shouted back the fisherman, "I'll do the rest."

Geoff smiled and leapt forward to grab the net. Gail stood back holding tightly to Mabel who was very excited about all the commotion and wondered if it would result in her getting that piece of bread she'd eyed up earlier.

"Here, let me help, you've got your hands full," said Geoff trying to work out how to extend the net to give him more reach. He managed to extend it as far as it would go and felt it starting to bend at the end.

The fisherman was torn between keeping control of his prize and risking losing it.

"Alright, don't wave it about man, put the net in the water and come stand right beside me. Watch me bring the fish towards it!"

Geoff steadied himself and pushed the net into the water. He was surprised how deep it was so close to the edge and kept pushing down until he hit what he thought was the bottom.

"Ok now here she comes, ease the net out a bit further," said the fisherman, his eyes focused on his work.

Geoff tried to pull the net up but it had got caught on something and wouldn't move.

"Come on man, it's coming in, where's the net gone?" he shouted, panic starting to take over his so far controlled voice.

"It seems to have got stuck," confessed Geoff and started to pull harder.

"You idiot!" bellowed the fisherman. "I can't hold it much longer. This is the monster of Lakeside View, it's never been caught and it's mine!"

Geoff gave one more tug and the net burst free causing him to lose his balance and stumble towards the fisherman.

"What the…"

Before the fisherman had time to finish his sentence, Geoff collided into him and made a grab for his arm. Geoff caught hold but he too was off balance and they both knew what was coming next.

They plunged head first into the lake with a synchronised splash.

"Dad, dad!" shouted Gail. Mabel began barking frantically and pulled her to the fisherman's peg where his maggot box had been knocked over, the contents rolling around with the odd one dropping into the water.

Geoff and the fisherman both emerged headfirst to the surface together and a spurt of water came out of both their mouths, reminding Gail of the fountain in their local park. Although that was two boys having a wee but still, it made her chuckle inside, now she knew her dad was alive.

The two men could just stand up with their chins touching the water. The fisherman turned his head towards Geoff and glared, his eyes burning with rage.

"I'm gonna kill you!!" he screamed. He raised his right hand out of the water and was still holding approximately half of his fishing rod, the other half having snapped off in the fall, taking the monster fish with it (or maybe the other way round).

"Hey mate, I was only trying to help," bumbled Geoff. "That net of yours was too long and…"

"Arrrrghh!" exclaimed the fisherman and lunged towards Geoff.

Now if you've ever lunged in water, it usually takes around three times longer to get where you want to be. This gave Geoff enough time to step gingerly to the side, leaving the fisherman to take his second plunge into the water.

"Dad, get out of the water while he's down there!" shouted Gail.

"Geoff began running *[picture someone running on the moon]* as fast as he could towards the bank. Realising he was still holding the net, he held it out for Gail to grab and pull him, taking his running speed up to a slow walk.

Gail grabbed the net end, dropping the lead in the process, releasing Mabel to devour the piece of bread she'd been desperate for. Disappointingly, it was very hard and crunchy, not what she'd hoped for but the thought disappeared as she discovered a plastic tub of luncheon meat and quickly worked her way through it.

Geoff finally climbed onto the bank just as the fisherman found his feet again. He then proceeded to flap his hands like a wild goose, splashing the water over and over in a crazed sort of dance move you see an entertainer perform at a children's 5th birthday party.

"I'll get you, you….I'll find out where you live!" These were the last words Geoff and Gail heard as they grabbed Mabel's lead, tugging her away from licking the final remnants of meat from the tub, and headed back to their pitch and the safety of Woody and Janice.

Chapter 20

Janice was just returning from the facilities which she was mighty impressed with. She had devised a rating system in her head for cleanliness and services and these were a good 9 out of 10. You only got a 10 if you had Dyson hairdryers and that accolade would have to wait for another trip!

As she looked up she saw Geoff, Gail and Mabel running towards her. It reminded her of Daniel Day Lewis in the movie The Last Of The Mohicans when he was being pursued by, well, Mohicans. She put her hand over her eyes to shield the evening sun and could have sworn she saw water dripping from Geoff.

"Not again," she murmured under her breath. "Please not again…"

Janice climbed into Woody and peered through the window. They were approaching fast and sure enough, Geoff was soaked through.

Janice rolled her eyes and waited in anticipation for the story this time.

As they got to the habitation door, Geoff glanced over

to pitch 12 and saw Brian and his wife Bev sipping gin and tonics.

"Looks like someone's been for a dip," shouted Brian and they both raised their glasses.

Gail climbed into Woody first with Mabel at her feet. Janice thought she could see something round her mouth but parked that thought.

"Dad fell in the lake and took a fisherman with him. He was really mad, I think he's gonna kill dad."

Janice's expression froze as Geoff climbed through the habitation door.

"Stop there man, you're dripping wet!" shouted Janice. "What the hell has happened?"

"You're not going to believe this…"started Geoff.

"Oh yes I am!" snapped Janice. Twice in two weeks, what is it with you and water?!"

Gail looked puzzled. "Why what else has…? Oh god, the motorhome show! Was that you dad? Oh no, what will my friends say when they find out it's my dad? I'm ruined!"

"Hold on, I nearly drowned out there trying to do a good deed. What about me?" retorted Geoff, as water trickled down his arms and legs. He could have sworn there was something moving in his pants but he daren't check at this point. Instead, he continued telling the tale.

"There was this fisherman and he had caught a fish. Well not quite, and he needed me to hold the net. It got stuck and somehow we both fell in. I don't think it was still on his line…"

"Oh good grief. We've not been here one night and we're likely to be evicted!" gasped Janice. "Does he know where our pitch is?"

"I don't think so," said Geoff. We left him in the water. I think he was trying to find the end of his rod so it bought us a bit of time. Oh, and Mabel ate all his bait too so we need to watch her belly."

"That's all we need," said Janice. "Well, get to the showers man, not that you need any more water but at least it will be clean. Here, take these."

"Can't I use ours?" asked Geoff. "Then no one will see me like this."

"No, I'm not having you mess up my nice clean bathroom. Here, off you go!"

Janice handed Geoff a towel, shower gel and deodorant and shuffled him out of the door. Mabel went to sit down in the front cabin. She wasn't quite feeling herself and needed a rest after all the excitement.

Janice and Gail sat down at the dining table.

"Did dad really do that at the motorhome show mum? There was loads of damage and everyone wants to know who did it!" Gail said desperately.

"Yes, it was your father. If I told you the whole story, you wouldn't…ok yes you might believe it as you've known him all your life. All we can hope is they haven't got CCTV of the incident."

"That man was really angry mum. He said the fish was the biggest in the lake and had never been caught. Some sort of legend and all that."

"That's all we need. Well, we need to lay low tonight," said Janice. "Let's choose a DVD to watch, it'll keep your father under control."

"Too right" said Gail. "That fisherman had a big knife down there. What if he came here in the night?"

"Mabel will have him," said Janice glancing at the cocker spaniel who was looking a bit sorry for herself.

"What's wrong with you then, eh? Belly a bit funny?"

Little did she know.

Chapter 21

The evening passed quietly. Geoff returned from the facilities without incident and made up the double bed from the lounge seating in the back of Woody. Gail was having the dropdown bed nearer the front as the tv was at the back and Geoff and Janice thought she'd be up all night watching if they took the front and more comfy sleeping option.

They all settled down to watch The Truman Show while Mabel lay unusually silently in her bed. Sharing bags of mini chocs were handed round and they all inwardly loved the fact they were outside but inside enjoying a movie together. Here was another reason this life was so good.

The film finished around 10pm with Geoff wondering how someone had no idea they were on a tv show all their life and ended up driving a boat into a wall that looked like the horizon.

"Well, you wouldn't find me falling for all that," said Geoff confidently.

"If you had been in that film, they'd have had you adopted at birth and chosen another kid," laughed Janice.

"Imagine the mayhem you would have caused, ending up in a boat with all that water around. You'd have been over the side in no time!"

Gail laughed out loud *[that's a lol I think]* and Geoff pulled a face. He always did that when he couldn't come back with something he thought was funnier.

"Ha ha." He said sarcastically. "Well we'd better take Mabel out for her last walk. Come on girl!"

Mable stood up and felt her tummy make some strange noises inside. She looked at Geoff sheepishly and turned around in a circle twice and lay back down.

"I don't think she feels too good after eating all that fish food," Geoff said, kneeling down to stroke her head. "Maybe we wait until morning, give her time to sleep it off."

"I hope you're right," said Janice. "This is a small space…"

[Now then, time for a bit more advice. When you're in a motorhome, even quite a big one, you need to manage movements carefully. Everyone can't be in the same place at the same time, it doesn't work. For example, Woody's kitchen is opposite the bathroom door, so if you want the bathroom, you can't be washing up – get it?]

Janice organised Geoff and Gail to sort out the dropdown bed at the front while she was in the bathroom. Janice sat at back on their bed scrolling through the tv channels for something to watch before lights out.

During the next 15 minutes, they all took turns in getting ready for bed and it kind of just…worked. Mabel watched them all shift around in relays from the comfort of her bed and hoped she would get her appetite back in the morning.

"Nothing to watch," said Janice, "even with all these channels. Anyway, I'm shattered, what a day!"

"Yes babe, me too" said Geoff. "I'm sure we'll have a quieter day tomorrow."

"I won't hold my breath" whispered Janice.

"Gail, I'm turning the Wi-Fi off so phone away now please, you need your sleep!"

"Awww dad!" cried Gail, "just 10 more minutes. Kimberley Hodgson is telling us about her blind date and just got to the bit where she punched him."

"Good grief" said Geoff. "Right, 10 minutes and that's it."

Chapter 22

Geoff turned over and pulled his pillow around the top of his head. Then he pulled it down further over his nose. For some reason, that didn't seem to satisfy his comfort, why was that?

He opened his eyes and, for a split second, had no idea where he was. He'd never looked up at the ceiling that now looked down on him or the blinds that presumably covered the windows, leaving the room very but not completely black.

Then it hit him, the overwhelming smell of… well… sick. It brought back memories of his early nights out when he spent the end of the evening hugging the bowl of someone's toilet. Then he thought of the night Janice drank too much Australian wine and didn't make it to the bathroom in time, as she could only crawl on all fours to get there.

He switched on the small light above his head and sat up.

"Janice, Janice, Janice!" he said, his voice getting louder with each prod in her side as he waited for a response.

"Uurrghh, what's the matter?" mumbled Janice. "Is it burglars? Mabel will get them…oh my god, what's that smell?!!"

As if revived by smelling salts on a rugby field, Janice sprang upright in bed and put her hand over her mouth.

"That is bad!" she exclaimed.

Geoff got out of bed and put on the middle interior light that lit up the kitchen section of Woody.

"I can't see any…urrrgh no, I've stood in it!"

Now Janice has quite a bad gag reflex, many people do, and the smell, combined with the thought of whatever it was squishing between Geoff's toes was too much and she leapt from the bed, pushed passed him and jumped into the bathroom.

Geoff heard familiar sounds coming from their brand new bathroom and he knew then it was going to be a long night.

Just then, Mabel came out from her little place near the front of Woody and wagged her tail frantically at Geoff. She felt much better after parting with that strange stuff she ate by the lake and was now ready for a nice walk.

"Mabel, no. Look what you've done. Oh no, I can hardly stand it!"

Mabel hung her head and looked for mum for support. She wasn't there so she decided to jump onto mum and dad's bed to find her. Sniffing the bed she realised which side was mum's and shuffled herself over the other side, turned around three times and curled up right where Geoff's head had been 5 minutes earlier.

"Great" said Geoff, "lost my bloody bed too now!"

"What's all the noise? Oh what's that smell. Dad is that

you?" Gail was now awake, no mean feat for someone who could sleep through Armageddon.

"Mabel's been sick and now your mother's being sick. Don't you start girl!" exclaimed Geoff.

"Well clean it up quickly, I can't sleep with all this noise. Sleep is good for the skin you know and I've got a spot the size of Yorkshire on my chin."

"I'm not coming out until it's gone!" shouted Janice from the inner sanctum of the tiny bathroom. "I'll only start again!"

Geoff sighed. This was not how he planned his first night in Woody.

One of the few talents recognised by his family was his ability to clean up in circumstances like this. He braced himself and went to work.

Half an hour later, Woody was clean, if still a little whiffy. Janice was back in bed, and Gail had fallen asleep again.

Geoff made them both a cup of tea and shuffled Mabel down the bed as he got in beside Janice.

"I knew she wasn't right. Why did you let her eat all that rubbish?" said Janice sipping her tea.

"I didn't. I was six foot under water at the time woman, wrestling with Captain Ahab!" Geoff said, taking a gulp from his Dad's Motorhome cup.

Janice scowled and then laughed. "Life is never dull with you Mr Watt is it?"

"No one knows what cards they'll be dealt," said Geoff. "You just have to make the most of 'em."

"Oh you certainly do that. We need to watch out for that fisherman tomorrow. He'll be on the lookout for you."

"Yes, maybe we should head out for the day. You could bring your sketching stuff and Gail can get on her bike. If we are off site, he'll not find us."

"Not us, you man!" said Janice.

They sat for a while in silence, both reflecting on their adventurous day. Geoff thought about his chat with Gail and smiled. Janice thought about nearly being run over by Woody and scowled. They both began storing their own recollections into their memory bank for another day.

"I wonder if he still had the fish on his line," said Geoff thoughtfully. "If he didn't, it's a great story for the one that got away!"

"Well, let's just hope you're the one that got away by the time we leave this place," said Janice and finished her cuppa. "Come on, let's get back to sleep. Big day tomorrow."

"Yep, as Lindsey Buckingham sang "Don't stop thinking about tomorrow, don't stop thinking about…"

Janice stopped him in his tracks with three short sharp kisses.

"That'll do! Night night."

"Night night Mrs W".

Out went the lights and they settled down to sleep.

There was a calmness to the silence. Being outside but inside was different and somehow felt more reassuring than just being at home in bed.

A burp shattered the silence.

"Mabel, off the bed!" proclaimed Geoff and Mabel jumped down and skulked off into her own bed for the rest of the night.

Chapter 23

Geoff woke first and quickly realised why. He needed a wee. The prostate tablets were good. He didn't get up half as much as he used to, but that first wee was a usually a whopper. He turned and saw Janice was still asleep.

"Good" he thought. "Glad she's got a good rest after all that last night."

He walked towards the bathroom and Mabel lifted her head and motioned to get up.

"Not yet Mabel," whispered Geoff as loud as he could. You can have a wee after me," and he opened the bathroom door, went in and closed it behind him.

He looked around their new bathroom, now even more sparkling from his clean up job after Janice's episode. There was still a hint of lasagne in the air and Geoff quickly tried to put the events of last night out of his head.

It really was home from home, but he then felt a little shudder when he remembered his bathroom hell in the *Gladiator 1000*. He hoped that was the end of it but then remembered Stu had said they were hopeful they would find the culprit.

A few minutes later [it takes a while when you have a dodgy prostate], he was walking Mabel around the campsite, taking a look at the different shapes and sizes of the vehicles. He wasn't really interested in caravans although Janice was. He liked to see the other motorhomes, what accessories they had, and what he could google when he got back home.

They passed one small campervan and Geoff noticed a couple of fishing rods leaned up against the side of the van. To his horror, he saw two more, much smaller rods next to them and realised they were two halves of a broken rod.

"Pitch 25," thought Geoff. "Won't come this way tomorrow."

"Mabel, come on!" he said as loudly and quietly as he could and jerked her lead as she dug her heels in. She was very upset as she'd discovered a very interesting patch of wee that she hadn't finished sniffing. She reluctantly left it, for hopefully another time.

As he walked along he realised how much he enjoyed this morning walk before most of the other campers had risen from their slumber. The quiet serenity made Geoff feel quite calm and he breathed in deeply to taste the fresh Cumbrian air.

Ahead of him he spotted a large chap coming his way. Alongside was a tiny looking dog with long ears on a lead as thin as a shoestring. Geoff thought it looked quite novel – a big guy with a little pooch. As he got nearer, Geoff realised the man looked a bit familiar.

It was Bouncer Dave, the one from the motorhome show.

As they approached each other, Dave looked up and Geoff could tell his face gave away a feeling of dread. Bouncer Dave's eyes moved quickly from left to right, trying to find an escape route but all he saw were pitches fully occupied and offering no way out.

"Morning," said Geoff as he approached Dave. "Aren't you the guy from the show we went to?"

"Ummm, no. Errr, yeh. Not sure," bumbled Dave.

"Yes I remember, you were on the door, checked our tickets. What are you doing here?"

As the two men had stopped, Mabel decided to check out the little dog with the pointy ears. As she went to inspect its rear end, as all dogs do as a civilised meet and greet, the little pooch snarled and snapped at her, taking her completely by surprise.

"Talula! Stop it!" shouted Dave.

"Talula?" thought Geoff. "Well would you have thought it."

Mabel backed off and decided it was safer to explore a bit of grass where it looked like some cooking had taken place. She smelled cooked meat and started to follow her nose towards a table a few feet away. Geoff pulled her back but she realised each time she tugged her way, she got a bit closer.

"I've done a few motorhome shows now and thought all these people can't be wrong so a couple of years ago I got myself a little campervan and me and Talula take trips here and there when I'm not working. Can't beat it." Dave said very matter-of-factly.

"You're right there" said Geoff. "Best thing we did buying our van, Woody he's called. First trip away and loving every minute". Geoff recounted the events so far since they left home and mulled them over in his head. He pulled Mabel back again as she pulled him towards the nearby pitch.

"You just don't know what will happen. Every trip is different," he said thoughtfully.

"Well I had to take a few days off after that last show, what with all that carnage when some idiot flooded the showcase motorhome. The panic that followed really stressed me out. Doc thinks I've got PDSA," said Dave looking at his hands as if expecting them to start shaking.

"Yeh, dreadful business" said Geoff, trying to work out what PDSA stood for. "I doubt they'll find out who did it though now."

"Oh well I heard the CCTV wasn't much help but apparently they've got some other evidence that shows something but don't know what."

"Really, I wonder what that can be?" said Geoff racking his brain.

"Anyway, I need to get Talula back for her breakfast," said Dave. "She gets a bit tetchy if you leave her waiting too long."

"Good grief," thought Geoff after he'd seen it go for Mabel. "Wouldn't like to get on the wrong side of that one!"

"Yeh, me too. Enjoy your stay." And with that, Geoff turned to Mabel who was slowly pulling him towards a camping table.

"Mabel, what are you doing girl!" shouted Geoff.

Mabel saw her chance as Geoff moved towards her and leapt under the table. To her delight she found two half eaten sausages and a few chips and quickly manoeuvred round the table legs to hoover them all up.

Her weaving now meant she was completely tangled up under a table leg and Geoff bent down to free her lead.

"Oi, what you playing at!" came a voice from the caravan on the pitch and an angry faced man came out of the doorway.

"Julie, someone is stealing our picnic table. Oi, I'll report you to the warden!"

"No I'm not, the dog just got tangled under it and I'm trying to get her out. You must be messy eaters 'cos there's food all over the floor." Geoff now wished he hadn't said that as the man came storming towards him.

"Are you calling my kids messy eaters?!" growled the man who up close looked like he had a regular gym membership.

"Errr, well, no" stuttered Geoff. "I didn't know you had kids," and then regretted that too.

"So you think me and the missus are messy eaters?! I'll give you…"

Luckily Geoff freed Mabel just as the man came within feet of them both.

At the same time, Bouncer Dave had heard the commotion and returned to the scene.

"Is this guy troubling you?" he said to Geoff. Now Dave was even bigger than the angry man so this could have been an interesting contest but Geoff felt it was a bit early in the day for a Sky Box Office boxing match.

"No, not really," he said more confidently and backed away hurriedly onto the pathway that led all round the site. "Mabel was just tidying up after him."

"Ok, show's over," said Dave sternly looking at the man with piercing eyes.

The man looked Dave up and down and then at Talula. This guy was a giant but the dog?! Baffled, he put his hands up, shook his head and turned around to walk back to his caravan.

"Some people!" said Geoff with his nose in the air. "We come away for a quiet time and they just don't know how to act."

"Yeh," said Dave pensively, wondering just how much that little altercation had to do with him.

"Well, see you and try not to get into any more trouble." And with that he walked away with Talula yapping at his heels, demanding her breakfast immediately.

"Ok poppet," Geoff heard him say and realised who wore the trousers in that household.

Chapter 24

Back at the pitch, Geoff tied Mabel to the ground hook, another special buy from the internet, and saw activity in the kitchen. The smell of bacon and the sound of the sizzle of a frying pan made his taste buds tingle.

Janice was preparing a full English and Geoff felt he was in heaven. He jumped up into Woody and shook off his sandals.

"Morning gorgeous, I love you." He said.

"Morning darling, I love you too," said Janice and they gave each other their three short sharp kisses to start the day.

"You are my best wife ever!" said Geoff proudly.

"I know," Janice said, recalling Geoff's difficult divorce after they had met. He and his first wife had split up two years before but it had taken some time to sort everything out and it had been very stressful for Geoff.

"Would you say the same if I gave you a bowl of granola?" she chuckled, knowing Geoff's love of food and her cooking really were a match in heaven.

"Oh yes my dear," he said, secretly praying she never made him eat granola.

"Gail? Wake up lass!" he shouted and poked the duvet on the dropdown bed.

"Urrrrr, gerroff!" came a grumbly voice. "What time is it?"

"8 o'clock. Time for breakfast. You don't sleep in on campsites, everyone's up and about by now."

"Blooming 'eck dad!" cried Gail "It's the crack of dawn!"

"Well, you'll get no bacon if you don't get up." said Janice turning the rashers in the pan.

Now the only thing Gail liked more than chocolate was bacon and with that she sprung up and breathed in the smoky aroma.

"Ok, ok. Dad get out of the way, I neeeeed bacon!"

Geoff headed to the back of Woody and sat on their bed while Gail got down from hers and headed into the bathroom. *[As noted before, negotiating space in a motorhome is very important to keep everyone sane.]*

"Guess who I saw on our walk. That ticket guy from the motorhome show." said Geoff.

"Never, what a small world!" exclaimed Janice putting the bacon into the oven below the hob to keep warm with the sausages, while she cracked open the eggs. She was very pleased with all the cooking facilities in Woody – proper home from home she thought.

"He had a tiny pooch called Talula, unbelievable!. He also said he thought the authorities had some other evidence about that bit of trouble at the show." Geoff continued nervously.

"Oh" said Janice, "I wonder what that could be."

"I think they're bluffing" said Geoff. If they've no CCTV, they can't prove who it was."

"No, I suppose not" said Janice, rather unconvincingly. "Well, just the eggs to finish. Put the toast on will you?"

Fifteen minutes later, they were sat outside in the early morning sun eating their full English and sipping their orange juice.

"This is the life," said Geoff. He saw Brian emerge from his motorhome opposite and gave him a wave. Brian returned the wave as he headed towards reception.

"That's what I like about this life" said Geoff. "Meeting people, all sorts of people. You get people from all walks of life and they all come to the countryside to enjoy themselves, like they all have a common purpose."

"Yes, they do come to enjoy themselves but try telling that to that fisherman yesterday," said Janice, looking at Gail who rolled her eyes and took another large bite on her bacon buttie.

"Never been so embarrassed," Gail said "And that's saying something with dad!"

"Ay, young lady, I was trying to help. If it's not appreciated, I might not offer next time," said Geoff defensively.

"God help us if there's a next time dad. That man is after your blood!"

Geoff thought of the angry man this morning and then reconsidered his statement about meeting people. He decided not to tell them about Mabel's encounter with the picnic table.

"Well some folk are just a bit tense," he said. "They

need to chill out a bit more. That's the whole point of coming out here."

"You hurled him into the water, made him lose a prize fish and broke his rod dad. It probably cost a fortune. He looked like a proper angler, or whatever they're called."

"Nah," said Geoff, thinking about all the rods lined up at pitch 25. "Just an amateur I reckon."

"Well, no more helping this holiday Geoff," said Janice. "People can only take so much of your generosity. Finish your black pudding. We'll get tidied up and then I want to go for a nice walk and find somewhere to sketch."

As Geoff and Janice washed up the breakfast things, Gail went off for a ride on her bike. It was a relief for Geoff and Janice to see her separated from her phone and doing something that didn't involve technology.

They understood it was the normal thing now and they had grown up in a very different world, but there was no doubt it had put a huge strain on the younger generations who saw social media as the standard by which they judged themselves. Gail was pretty sensible but even she was so absorbed in it all, they couldn't help but worry.

"Good to see her out on her bike," said Geoff.

"I know," agreed Janice. "It sometimes feels they live in another world at that age and we are on the outside. You see the damage every day in the media, especially for girls but how can you stop them?"

Geoff thought a bit while he dried a plate. He had worked in technology in his previous job and saw the benefits but also the darker side and almost addictive qualities it brought.

"I don't think you can stop them love. You just have to help them manage it."

Janice nodded and felt quite proud of her husband's common sense for once. She loved him for his heart of gold and good intentions but knew it was sometimes his downfall. That said, she wouldn't change him, not for the world!

Chapter 25

Soon Woody was ship shape and Mabel was getting excited, seeing her lead in mum's hand. Geoff gathered together a few bits into a small backpack, along with Janice's sketching pad and materials.

"Well, all ready" he said. "Let's go see what Lakeside View has to offer. Come on Mabel!" Mabel grabbed her ball and put it in front of Geoff.

"Not now Mabel, we'll take it with us," said Geoff and popped the ball into the rucksack. They locked up Woody just as Gail returned on her bike with another girl in tow.

"This is Milly," said Gail. "We're going to explore a bit."

"Hi Milly," said Geoff and Janice in stereo.

"Ok love. Enjoy yourself. We'll be back around 3ish. Here's a spare key for Woody if you get back first. Don't lose it!" said Janice in a tone Gail recognised as deadly.

"I won't," she said and tucked it safely in her bag strapped around her like a sash. "Milly's into Black Widow big time so we're gonna compare notes."

"Ok, well don't be on your phone all the time!" warned Janice looking at Geoff for support.

"Yes, keep off that Instaface!" said Geoff and returned the look to Janice to see if he'd succeeded. Janice rolled her eyes.

Milly looked at Gail with a 'what IS he on about?' expression and Gail just shrugged.

"Ignore my dad. He thinks he knows about technology but he doesn't. He can't even work the firestick remote and it only has five buttons."

"Bit like my dad," said Milly and with that they turned their bikes around and headed off down the roadway.

"Cheeky mares!" said Geoff looking at Janice, but got no support.

Geoff and Janice walked through the campsite as the sun began to warm up nicely. Geoff took note of one or two interesting accessories, in particular a nice windbreak that a chap was BBQing behind.

"Must check that out when I get back," he thought.

Janice looked at him and read his mind.

"Don't be buying loads of stuff we don't need man!" she said.

"What do you mean woman? I'm only window shopping," he replied, smiling to himself.

Towards the back of the site there was a dog walk that led to some woods. They took the path and about half a mile later found themselves in a beautiful glade with the sun flickering through the branches and leaves above them.

"This is gorgeous!" said Janice. I think I might park myself here on this big stone and do some sketching. I've got my paints so I can capture some of the colours while I'm here."

"Great idea," said Geoff taking her cushion and artist stuff out of the backpack. "I'll carry on with Mabel and see where this leads. I might be able to let her off further on. We haven't seen anyone for a bit."

"Ok, well just watch out with her, you know what she's like."

Mabel looked at mum and dad clearly talking about her and waited for the ball to emerge from the bag.

"See you in a bit," said Geoff and he and Mabel headed further into the woods.

Janice settled herself on her cushion and looked around for the best angle to begin. It really was a picturesque little spot. Just what she loved capturing in her own way. She found the perfect scene and began.

Chapter 26

Geoff and Mabel continued on their journey and eventually came to a drystone wall with a stile. Geoff looked over the wall and saw a field that sloped up quite steeply in the middle and then steeply down the other side so you couldn't really see the other half of it from where Geoff was stood, as it disappeared out of view. He then looked at Mabel.

"I'm going to have to carry you over this girl if we are going to continue our adventure," he said.

Geoff picked up Mabel, staggering a little as he'd forgotten just how chunky she was now.

"Bloomin' 'eck!" he puffed. "We need to cut down on those night time snacks Mabel." Mabel grunted as Geoff heaved her over the stile and into a field that had a narrow path down the right hand side.

Next to the wall was a giant trough full of water that appeared to have been there for ages.

"Probably when it was used as a cow field or something," Geoff thought.

He turned his nose up at the smell that was emanating

from the trough and told Mabel not to try and drink the water.

Just ahead of them there was the start of the narrow pathway to the right of the field with a rickety handmade sign.

"Cross field with care. Beware of the birds!" Geoff muttered to himself. The words were painted in red with a drawing of a skull and crossbones that looked like it had been painted by Gail when she was in Year 3.

Geoff looked across the field and saw two large crows dancing around cawing at each other. "This farmer is a right joker Mabel! Who's afraid of a couple of crows!"

Mabel looked at him and had no idea what he was saying. She was desperate to be let off the lead so she could chase her ball.

"When is the ball coming out?" she said over and over in her head.

They continued on sticking to the path, until they reached just before the middle the field. Geoff looked around and couldn't see anyone or anything in sight.

"Ok Mabel, just a few throws of the ball and then we'll head back," he said and pulled the ball out of the rucksack he'd taken off his back. Mabel jumped up and down with gusto, urging dad to throw it.

Geoff threw the ball and Mabel scampered after it. Back she came and Geoff tossed it a bit further in a different direction. Of she went and back she came, this time with the ball and a bit of foliage in her mouth.

Ten throws later and Geoff was running out of different directions to throw it. He decided to throw it a bit further to mix things up a bit. He threw the ball as far as he could and it bounced up the slope, over the top and out of view.

Mabel was sharp and in hot pursuit. She ran up to the middle of the field and then disappeared over the hill.

Geoff waited for her to return. He thought she was a bit longer than he expected and started to feel a bit concerned.

"Mabel! Mabel! Come on, where are you?" he shouted.

Suddenly she appeared from over the hill, racing towards him faster than he'd ever seen, ball in mouth.

Geoff was about to praise her when next over the hill came two huge birds at pace. Geoff froze and stared in amazement. He imagined the scene from Jurassic Park, the one where all the dinosaurs are running down the hill after Sam Neil (he thought that was the one but there's been so many films now) and suddenly came back to his senses.

"Emus? What the…run Mabel run!" he shouted as the birds gained ground on her.

Geoff suddenly realised he too was in the field and started to run back towards the wall and stile they had used to get in. He ran as fast as he could, hearing Mabel closing in on him and the thundering feet of the two big birds getting louder and louder.

In a few seconds, Mabel overtook Geoff and seemed very clear where the exit was. Geoff looked behind him and saw the emus gaining on him quickly.

"Who keeps emus in the Lake District?" he shouted to himself, huffing and puffing. He realised he'd lost some ground turning round and decided to keep focused on the wall where the stile was.

Mabel reached the wall and clambered up the wooden stile, finding her way through the middle of it where the gap was just big enough for her to squeeze through on her own. She knew danger when she saw it and now it was every dog for itself!

Geoff saw her scramble through and felt relieved she was out of harms way. At the very same second, he knew he wasn't anywhere near safe yet and looked for another gear in his legs. It wasn't there but now he was just a few feet away from the wall as the thundering feet of the two enormous birds came closer and closer. He could have sworn he could smell them as he reached the end of the path.

He climbed onto the stile just as one of the emus caught him up and that slight delay gave it the opportunity it needed to reach out and peck him on the bum.

"Oooow!" cried Geoff and turned around to prevent any further pecks. By now the second emu had arrived and, standing half way up the stile, he saw just how tall they were. They stopped and stared at Geoff cocking their heads to one side as they weighed up their next move.

Geoff stopped too and for a few seconds, their was a Mexican stand off like in those old westerns, when the good guy has a showdown in the street of some dirty old town with the big bad guy and they both are waiting to reach for their guns.

Geoff remembered he had a couple of apples in his rucksack and wondered if he could create a distraction while he got away.

"Ok, nice birdies, who'd like a nice crunchy apple then?" he stuttered the words out as politely as he could.

Slowly he took the bag off his back, unzipped the pocket and felt around until he found one of the apples.

He waved it up and down and was pleased to see the emus heads pop up and down and left and right like synchronised swimmers, following the apple's movements.

"That's it!" said Geoff carefully feeling more in control. "Who wants a nice juicy apple?" And he then launched it over the top of the two birds with all his might.

To his relief both turned around to see where the apple had landed. To his horror, only one ran in that direction. The other turned back round to face Geoff and took a few slow steps towards him.

Just as he started to reach in the bag for the second apple, the bird suddenly stretched out its long neck and grabbed at the back pack, grabbing hold with an incredibly tight grip. Geoff began pulling it back and seeing him struggling, Mabel began to bark frantically from the other side of the wall.

Geoff now knew he was in a tug of war with a giant bird standing on a stile in the middle of nowhere and briefly wondered how this could happen to him. As he tugged one way, the bird tugged the other until the bird had turned him almost ninety degrees, his back now facing the stone trough that stood next to the stile.

With one big pull, Geoff managed to release the rucksack from the emu's grip and for a nano-second remembered with pride the tug-o-war match he helped win on his school sports day in his last year at primary school.

The image then quickly vanished as he realised he was losing his balance as his momentum kept going backwards.

Before he could utter any words, he fell backwards and landed in the stone trough full of dirty water.

The bag fell to the side and the emu nuzzled inside it finding the second apple. Satisfied with it's find, it turned around and headed away to join its partner in crime, leaving Geoff spluttering and waving his arms about, trying to grab hold of the sides of the trough. It was deeper than it looked but eventually he got a grip with both hands and pulled himself up to sit in the bath of stagnant water.

Thinking the coast was clear, Mabel scampered through the stile and looked for her dad, puzzled to see the rucksack on the floor. Geoff rose out of the trough like Neptune from the deep and Mabel was relieved to see her dad was safe and well. She dropped the ball and looked up at him, anticipating they would continue their game now the two big things with the long legs had gone away.

"Uuurrrggggh, this water stinks!" exclaimed Geoff as he picked pieces of grass and goodness knows what from his shirt and shorts.

Mabel caught a whiff of the smell, picked up the ball and headed back through the stile. Whatever had happened, that was not a good smell and not even playing fetch would make her want to get another whiff from dad.

Geoff clambered out of the trough and over the stile. Had that really just happened? What was he going to tell Janice? Oh god, he smelled really bad!

Chapter 27

Geoff and Mabel walked gingerly back through the shaded wood to where it opened out into the beautiful space they had left Janice in.

There she was, deep in her work. Geoff saw Janice ahead of them and managed a small smile. He knew Janice loved to paint and wished she believed in how good she really was. One day she will, he thought to himself.

Janice looked up when she heard some twigs crack and stopped sketching. Coming towards her was what she thought was her husband. But he had a green slimy tinge to his complexion and his short-sleeved white shirt was now a similar colour to his khaki shorts. He had something in his hair, straw perhaps?

"What on earth has happened now?" she gasped to herself.

Mabel ran up to her wagging her tail and dropped the ball – it was mum's turn to play now.

"Geoff Watt, what has happened to you? I let you go off for an hour and look at you!" she cried in disbelief.

"Janice, you won't believe it. We were attacked by two emus and…"

Janice stared at him, this time with a sense of despair. Yet again he was soaked to the skin. What was it about Geoff and water? But this wasn't any old water. The closer he got the more a terrible stench wafted into her nose.

"Stay there!" she shouted. "Oh my god, that is disgusting! Why are you all wet?"

"I fell in a trough..." was all Geoff could muster.

"Good grief man, what am I going to do with you. Well, that's the end of my relaxation," she said, picking up her sketch pad and pencils.

Geoff tried to get nearer to see what she had drawn.

"No! Stay back!" Janice exclaimed. "You're staying well away until we get you cleaned up."

They made their way back through the pretty wood until they reached the dog walk that took them back into the main campsite.

As they walked along the path, Bouncer Dave was walking Talula and heading their way.

"Alright," said Dave. As he approached Geoff and Janice, he put his hand over his mouth and stepped away to the other side of the walkway. He looked Geoff up and down, remembering a film called 'The Swamp Thing' he'd seen as a teenager.

"Don't ask!" said Janice, "just don't ask!"

Geoff held up a hand and gave a small wave to Dave. Even Talula turned her nose up and strutted past as quickly as she could. Mabel, now on her lead and resigned to the fact dad had ruined her ball game, trotted obediently by Janice's side, fully aware mum was not happy with dad.

They walked to the toilet block and stopped outside the entrance to the men's showers. There was a sign on the door saying 'cleaning in progress'.

"Brilliant!" cried Janice sarcastically. "Right, wait here and get yourself into there when they've finished cleaning and put your clothes in that plastic bag I put in the rucksack. I'll come back in 10 minutes with some fresh clothes!"

Geoff just nodded frantically. Now was not the time to question his wife's orders.

Just as she finished speaking, Roger emerged from the men's block with a mop and bucket. He saw Geoff and his face turned sour as if he had just sucked on a lemon.

"He's not going in there like that!" exclaimed Roger. "We've got an award for our facilities, five star you know. He's going to ruin them. He'll need hosing down first. You can use the dog wash round the corner."

And with that, he jumped into a little golf buggy parked in front of the block and headed off.

Just then Brian from pitch 12 appeared with his towel under his arm. He looked at Geoff and then at Janice and shook his head.

"Another wet one?" he said and chuckled as he headed into the freshly cleaned showers.

Janice shepherded Geoff around to the dog wash, took the rucksack from him and turned on the hose. The water was freezing as she hosed him up and down watching the debris from the trough wash away down the grate beneath his feet.

"Ooooh, aaaaah, that's freezing!" shouted Geoff, his teeth chattering.

"Shut up man!" said Janice. "If you want a hot shower, you need to grit your teeth and bear it!"

One or two campers, who had sussed out the cleaning times, were now heading to the showers. They slowed down and gawped as they witnessed the surreal scene of a woman hosing down a man in the dog wash area, while their dog sat watching at the side.

Janice held her head down, hoping no one would remember her face. She wondered how she had ended up right here, right now, in this situation. But as she looked at her husband slowly reappearing from under all the slime and dirt, she remembered life would be very dull without him and managed a tiny inward smile.

"That'll do" she said, turning off the tap and unhooking Mabel's lead from the hook labelled 'dog park' next to the wash area.

"Get cleaned up in there and I'll go get a towel and some clothes. You'll have to come out and get them though. I can't come in there."

Ten minutes later Geoff peeped out of the door at the entrance to the men's block and saw Janice waiting with a bag. She handed it over and caught a glimpse of his bare bum as he rushed back to the shower cubicle to get dressed.

"Geoff Watt, whatever did I see in you?" she laughed and headed back to Woody with Mabel in tow.

Chapter 28

Fully cleansed and smelling of sea salt and lemongrass shower gel, Geoff returned to their pitch just in time to hear Gail complaining to Janice.

"It's not working mum. Even if I wave it in the air!"

Geoff climbed up into Woody and witnessed Gail doing some sort of crazy rave dance, her arms stretched up in the air swaying side to side.

"What's not working love?" said Geoff and then saw the little MiFi thing in Gail's right hand.

"The Wi-Fi dad. I'm trying to watch the latest episode of Davina De Booty's Drag Arena and it keeps sticking when they send in the corgis."

Geoff had a momentary blank in his brain as he thought he'd just entered a different universe and then shook his head quickly from side to side.

"I have no idea what that means but give me that thing and I'll sort it."

Gail handed Geoff the miffy thing and continued to bounce up and down like a frenzied terrier. Geoff peered at the screen and gasped.

"You've used all the data!" he shouted "I got 10Gb and it's all gone! What have you been doing girl?"

"I've hardly used it" said Gail sheepishly. "Just watched a few episodes of Drag Arena and a couple of movies."

"Good grief, well that's done it. You'll have to wait until we get home tomorrow."

"I can't dad! Everyone will have seen it by then and talking about it. If Ginger Minger doesn't survive tonight, I'll have lost my bet!"

"Ginger what???!!!" exclaimed Geoff. "What is this programme Janice? Is it on Channel 5?"

"It's on the internet man, they don't have programmes there. It's all in a cloud."

"The world has gone mad," sighed Geoff and took out his phone. "Ok I'll top it up a bit but no more movie downloads!"

Ten minutes later Gail was happily watching Ginger Minger trapped in an arena singing Somewhere Over The Rainbow with twelve very large snakes, waiting to see if he/she/they could stay in there for the 10 minutes required to stay in the contest.

It was made even harder as the arena decreased in size, one foot every minute, meaning by the end of the time signalled by a loud hooter, there would be little space to click his/her/their silver thigh length boots together and shout 'there's no place like Davina De Booty's Drag Arena!'

In the meantime, Geoff had assembled his portable BBQ and set it alight.

"Pass me the burgers love!" he shouted to Janice who was busily toing and froing between Woody and the table, preparing everything for their Al Fresco meal.

"Here you go," said Janice as she handed him four quarter pounders. "Are you sure those coals are smokeless? There weren't many reviews on eBay."

"'Course they are love. They're special lightweight ones. It said they are ideal for BBQs and fire pits and you don't need any firelighters, just light the bag and off you go. I was a bit surprised nearly all the reviews were from people in Morocco and Uzbekistan but you can't go wrong for the price."

Geoff proudly put on his MasterChef apron (well not a real one but again, eBay is great for just about anything) and surveyed the pitches around them. Most of the other campers were settling down for their evening meals or sat having an aperitif.

"This really is the life, eh Janice? Can you get a beer for the head chef?" called Geoff. A few minutes later, Geoff was sipping a cold beer and decided to check if it was ready to begin his feast.

"Hhhmmm," frowned Geoff. "The bag's burned away but it's not very hot." He called to Janice who was arranging some flowers she'd picked in a vase on the carefully laid out camping table.

"It's hard to tell with no smoke," he muttered.

Geoff waited a few more minutes and still the coals didn't seem to be giving off enough heat. He looked over to Brian who had now also begun his BBQ and saw him squeeze some fluid onto his coals. Instantly they burst into flames and Brian looked very chuffed with himself.

Geoff looked down at his tepid coals and felt a tinge inadequate. Swallowing his pride, he ambled over to Brian.

"Hiya mate, see you've got yours going well. Mine's

playing up, think the coals are a bit dry. Any chance I could borrow a bit of your fluid?"

"Hi there, coals a bit dry? Not heard that one. Anyway, sure mate, but be careful, you only need a little squirt to get it going. And don't let anyone see you. Roger doesn't like people using lighter fluid, says it's a fire hazard."

With that clear warning, Brian handed the bottle of BBQ fluid over to Geoff.

Geoff returned to his BBQ, clutching the bottle under his arm to avoid anyone seeing. He unscrewed the lid off the bottle and squeezed a little fluid onto the coals, careful not to put too much. He waited and felt a surge of disappointment as it made very little difference.

He looked up and saw Brian disappear into his motorhome.

"A bit more can't do any harm," he said and turned the bottle upside down and gave it a hard squeeze. The fluid spurted out of the bottle at a tremendous speed like washing up liquid and soaked the coals completely. He gave it another squeeze, just for good luck.

Geoff waited and very slowly the coals began to crackle. He smiled to himself and put the lid back on the bottle and put it down on the floor next to him.

"Next stop, a Michelin restaurant for me!" he cried and sauntered up to Woody.

"All hotting up nicely babe," he said proudly. "Pass me the sausages too."

Janice emerged with a pack of pork sausages and glanced over Geoff's shoulder.

"Oh my god!" exclaimed Janice. "I thought you said it doesn't smoke?"

Geoff turned round and saw what could only be described as a thick chimney of smoke rising from the BBQ up into the air. As each second passed, the chimney got thicker and thicker and the smoke got blacker and blacker.

"Oh crikey!" shouted Geoff. "It must have reacted with the coals. Maybe they make them different in Morrocco."

"What must have reacted man?" replied Janice.

"Errr, the fluid I put on it. It wasn't getting hot so I borrowed some from Brian."

While Geoff gasped open mouthed at the black wall of smoke that was billowing from the BBQ, Gail joined Janice at the open door and pulled a face that matched the ones etched on her parents, leaving no one in any doubt that she was their genetic child.

"Do something man!" exclaimed Janice.

Geoff thought for a moment and then headed round to Woody's garage and produced a small collapsible bucket. He ran into Woody and began to fill it with water from the kitchen sink.

As the water filled, he heard what he thought was a car alarm going off. Still the water filled the bucket and another alarm started, followed by another and another. Soon the air was filled with the sound of alarms all around their pitch.

"What the…!" Geoff muttered to himself and turned off the tap as the bucket was now as full as he dared fill it without spilling it.

He stepped out of Woody to a scene of utter chaos which reminded him of an episode from Casualty. As the wind blew the smoke around he could see silhouettes of people running around their pitches.

One person was trying to take down washing from their rotary airer and another was tending to their little boy who was crying and complaining his eyes were sore with the smoke. Mabel had awoken from her slumber under the picnic table and was now running around, pulling her extendable lead to the max.

"Where's all that smoke from?" shouted one voice.

"My smoke alarm won't stop!" exclaimed another.

"Mine neither!" agreed another.

"It's ruining my glass of Bordeaux!" cried another.

The sound of smoke alarms was now deafening as the smoke, carried by the gentle breeze, swept across the campsite and the motorhomes, campervans and caravans of Lakeside View.

Chapter 29

Geoff ran to the BBQ with the bucket of water and didn't notice Mabel's extendable lead. He tripped forward and fell face first onto the grass followed by the bucket of water, which managed to empty all over his head.

As he lay wondering how he'd got there, he heard the familiar sound of a golf buggy. It pulled up in front of pitch No 13 and, through the smoke, he could see two occupants jump out.

In no time, one was pulling a hose pipe from a reel on the back and headed through the wall of smoke to tackle the offending BBQ. The other was turning a handle on a water tank lodged on the back of the buggy.

"Stand back everyone. I'm trained and armed!" Roger emerged through the smoke like a Marvel hero armed with his hose at the ready.

"Turn her on Brenda!" he shouted and Brenda pressed a button on the tank.

Water blasted out of the hose as Roger fought the smoking BBQ for all he was worth. Although he had passed his level 1 fire and safety course, which he attended at the Cumbrian Fire Brigade's annual fete, he didn't have the best aim and the water began shooting beyond the BBQ.

Geoff had now begun to get up, and as he got to his knees, he was hit by a cannon of water that sent him backwards and down again, this time onto his back.

By now, Janice had already grabbed Mabel and rushed into Woody and slammed the door shut. As Geoff looked up he saw three faces peering through Woody's front window as Janice, Gail and Mabel watched on, unsure whether to be horrified or embarrassed. Mabel began barking as she desperately wanted to protect her dad from the nasty man who was now standing over him, still firing water into his face.

"I might have known!" exclaimed Roger. "I knew you were going to be trouble from the moment you entered my reception. Never have I had to invoke my fire and safety level 1 certificate before. Well, except for when Mrs Higgins's toaster blew up, but she's a seasonal tourer and has a loyalty card."

"Turn it off you clown!" shouted Geoff. "I'm drowning!"

Roger looked around and aimed the hose at the smoking BBQ.

Two minutes later and the BBQ was well and truly drenched. The smoke was now clearing and the alarms were beginning to turn off.

"Ok Brenda, that's a rip! Turn her off!" commanded Roger and blew the end of the hose in a distinctly weird Clint Eastwood fashion.

Geoff got to his feet, drenched from head to foot.

"What have we got here then," said Roger as he reached down and picked up the bottle of lighter fluid.

"These are banned items Mr Watt. There's a fine to pay, you know. Brenda, how much for a violation of the BBQ rules? I think it's under section 2 sub section 2.1.2."

"That's right Roger, errr Mr Grimstone. Fifty pounds for a violation due to use or misuse of chemicals or inflammable liquids or substances of any type that cause heat, fire or smoke in a place of habitation." Brenda took a breath.

"Sub section 2.1.3 also states failure to keep control of your BBQ results in a further £30 fine and a ban from visiting the site for 1 year."

Brenda felt very pleased with herself. She always liked to please Roger, although he never seemed to notice in the way she hoped.

"Very good Brenda. You'll go far my girl." stated Roger. "I'll take payment tomorrow Mr Watt, when you leave here for the last time at 10am sharp!"

And with that Roger turned on his heels like a soldier on parade and marched back to the golf buggy.

Geoff could have sworn he saw him salute to Brenda as they both faced each other for a brief moment and then jumped back into the buggy and drove off.

He looked around and saw the faces of his neighbours staring at him angrily from every pitch within reach.

"Errrr, sorry!" shouted Geoff half-heartedly. "Dodgy coals. From Morrocco."

"Idiot!" he heard.

"Shouldn't let people like that in here!" said another voice.

"I'm glad he's all wet," said the little boy who could now see again. "We love Roger, we love Roger!"

"I did warn you," said a voice and Geoff turned to see Brian walking towards him.

"Lethal stuff this, especially if the coals have been soaked in dodgy chemicals. Can't believe you're all wet again mate." And with that he chuckled, picked up the bottle of fluid, and headed back to his BBQ and G & T.

"My steaks are nearly ready," he said over his shoulder. "Nice and well done, just the way we like them." Geoff was sure he heard another chuckle.

He sighed and turned around to see Janice open the habitation door. She looked him up and down and shook her head.

Get inside and get dried…again! I'll make some beans on toast for us all."

Geoff squelched up to Woody and up the step. He took off his soaked MasterChef apron and realised the printed logo had run so you couldn't now read what it said.

This wasn't to be his moment of BBQ glory, but there would be others.

He would return.

Chapter 30

Geoff awoke to the sound of birds tweeting and the rustle of leaves gently blowing in the wind. He closed his eyes again and sighed a happy sigh as it dawned on him he was waking up indoors but outdoors. This was part of his passion for motorhoming, he loved waking up to a new morning and hearing the wildlife around him.

Suddenly the serene moment was shattered by a door slamming. Not just a single slam but a sliding noise followed by a slam. He turned over and saw Janice was still fast asleep, her mouth slightly open and from which she made a low reverse snore type sound.

There it was again. Slide, slam. And again, slide, slam. Geoff was now fully awake and so was Mabel, who gave out a muffled woof, followed by a slightly louder one and then a proper fully blown WOOF!

"Alright Mabel, calm down," said Geoff as he got out of bed. Woody was very dark inside, even after the sun came up. The pull down shutters and curtains on the windows and skylights meant you had no idea if it was day or night. Only the birds had told Geoff morning had broken.

He opened the curtain and slowly pulled up the shutter. Across on pitch 18, he could see a young couple outside their campervan *[the ones like the Volkswagens or transits that you think will have surf boards sticking out the top]*. They were getting ready to leave.

As they packed each item, they opened the sliding door, put it inside and then promptly shut the door again until the next item was ready to pack away. Slide, slam. Slide, slam.

"Why don't they just leave it open?" wondered Geoff.

Mabel had wandered over and he saw the longing look she always gave at either breakfast or tea time.

"Ok, in a minute Mabel, you need a wee first." Geoff put her lead on and quietly exited Woody.

At the same time Brian was walking along the pathway, probably having been to the site shop judging by the loaf of bread in his hand and the newspaper tucked under his arm. He saw Geoff and detoured over.

"Morning," he said. "Dried out have we?"

Geoff rolled his eyes. "That muppet Roger had no business hosing me down like that. Who does he think he is?"

"Nero I think," chuckled Brian. "See the sliders are making an early exit."

"Sliders?" said Geoff curiously.

"Yeh, that's what we call 'em. Sliders. Campervanners are the sliders of camping. Door open, door closed, door open, door closed," repeated Brian and motioned his arms acting out the procedure in case Geoff wasn't sure how it happened.

"Why don't they just leave it open until they've packed up?" said Geoff.

"Beats me," replied Brian. "That's the mystery of the sliders." And with that he turned and headed across to his motorhome, swinging his loaf as he went.

After a short walk (Mabel's walks are always short in the morning as she knows once the wee and poo are done, she will be that bit closer to getting her brekkie), Geoff returned and surveyed their Al Fresco dining area.

The BBQ was on its side and caked in wet ash. The table was covered with a thin layer of ash and the flowers Janice had put on the table were in tatters on the ground, probably half eaten by whatever had come scavenging in the night. Geoff picked up the collapsible bucket and looked inside and saw daylight where something had chewed a hole through the bottom.

He sighed a soulful sigh. It could have been so different. He was hoping to impress his neighbours with his new BBQ and culinary skills but in the end, he had looked like a contestant on It's A Knockout, hammered into submission by the dreaded water cannon. [*For those who grew up after the 1970s, Google it and you'll see what fun was had back then in the name of competition.*]

He hooked Mabel on the ground hook and tidied round. As he was picking up the vase that had held the flowers, he heard a familiar voice.

"What goes around comes around eh?"

Geoff looked up to see the fisherman from the lake walking past with two rods and his tackle box.

"I was going to hunt you down like that carp, but when I heard all the alarms going off last night, I knew it must be you. I came over and joined the crowd. Very entertaining, should have sold tickets, I'd have paid to watch!"

Geoff grunted something illegible as the fisherman carried on walking.

"Hear it's an £80 fine? First one ever in Lakeside View. Think you'll hold that record for a long time. I told Roger about you breaking my prize rod. He was looking up the rule for fishing violations as I left reception. Dread to think what your weekend break's gonna have cost you."

And away he went to spend another day in search of the whopper of the lake.

"Good grief!" cursed Geoff and continued tidying up the aftermath of the Tsunami that had hit pitch no 13. Perhaps he knew now what Roger had meant about being 'unlucky for some'.

Chapter 31

The Watts ate their breakfast in silence. Cereal and orange juice. Janice had insisted there would be no cooking this morning and Geoff had not argued. She was desperate to leave as soon as possible before Geoff could reek any more havoc on this five star campsite. Would she dare leave a review? She had said she always would, wherever they went. Somehow she thought she'd ignore the request when it arrived in her inbox.

Janice checked round to ensure everything was secure while Geoff took the toilet cassette to empty at the Elsan point. *[That's a technical term for an outside toilet with no lid that you flush the contents of your cassette down. Even more technical is there is a short hose attached to a tap which you can use to rinse out the cassette to avoid any remnants clinging on – I won't go any further, I think you get it.]*

Geoff arrived at the Elsan point and realised it was opposite pitch 25 where the angry fisherman was staying.

"Lucky he's out," he thought and twisted the top of the cassette pipe and poured the contents down the bowl, turning his head away and peeking a little to ensure there was only liquid and the special dissolvable toilet paper *[ok enough now]*.

He balanced the cassette on the side of the bowl and inserted the hose into the end of the pipe ready to squirt water in for a good rinse. Strangely, the tap was a few feet away from the Elsan bowl and so the hose only just reached the inside of the pipe. *[This is not an uncommon challenge if you frequent Elsan points regularly].*

As he turned round to the tap, he now realised it was too far away for him to turn it on and hold it in the cassette at the same time. Geoff's brain tried to think of a logical solution to his dilemma but nothing inspirational came to mind. He looked round and decided the quicker the better.

"Right here goes," he said and turned on the tap, intending to quickly grab the hose and cassette in one movement to complete his cleaning routine.

Now if you've ever turned on a tap that isn't yours, you'll know there's always a chance the pressure is different. Sometimes higher, sometimes lower and what needs three turns at home can only need one turn somewhere else.

In his haste to get a good jet of water into the cassette he gave the tap four good turns and then turned himself to grab the utilities.

Unfortunately, Geoff wasn't as nimble as he thought and Cumbrian Water had decided two turns would be enough to simulate the power of a jet washer.

Under such force the hose sprang out of the pipe and began swirling around in the air like a snake fighting the spell of its charmer. It spun around at terrific speed spraying water everywhere but the intended target.

A young boy riding past on his bicycle was caught

in the cross fire which made him wobble just enough to change course and head straight towards pitch 25.

Geoff just had time to see the boy's bike ram straight into the last remaining rod leant up against the campervan and he winced at the sound of a loud snap as the rod gave way to the oncoming bike. The bike keeled over taking the boy with him. Then the crying began.

Geoff's face changed shape and his brain cogs whirred inside his head, unsure what he should do next. The wild water snake was out of control and he decided damage limitation was the order of the day.

He turned back to the hose and commenced what can only be described as the snake charmer's boogie as he tried to catch it and pin it down. The hose seemed to sense it had a new dance partner and proceeded to point itself directly at Geoff, it's water jet hitting him firmly in the face and then working its way down like that basement scene from the movie Dirty Dancing.

Geoff was now drenched from head to foot but managed to reach out and grab his slinky dance partner in a fierce clinch. He directed it into the pipe and completed his cleaning routine he'd so calmly set out to complete a few minutes earlier.

The boy's crying had now caught the attention of his parents who were in a very posh caravan just a few pitches down from No 25.

They came running over and picked their son up, dusting him down and checking for signs of damage. Geoff could see the boy telling them his story and they both turned to look at Geoff across the pathway that separated them.

Their faces told Geoff his dance routine was not going to score him high points and he quickly turned off the tap, grabbed the cassette and headed away from the scene as fast as he could. He felt his shirt and trousers cling to him as the water soaked through his clothing and ran down his legs into his socks and sandals *[Yes socks and sandals. You would be amazed at the clothing you witness on campsites]*.

He briefly looked back to see the dad waving his fist and shouting something like "I know who you are! You're that idiot who tried to burn down the site last night and set off our smoke alarm!"

Geoff made it back to Woody and put the cassette back in the holder. He waked round and opened the habitation door.

"Can you pass me a towel love?" he said gingerly.

Janice came to the door and stared at her husband. She had only let him out of her sight for five minutes. How on earth had he got so wet again? Had he fallen down the Elsan? God forbid he smelled bad again if she had to sit next to him all the way home.

"Don't tell me!" she exclaimed. "I do NOT want to know. Get in man and get dried. What is it with you and water?"

Geoff sheepishly climbed up into Woody and, as he turned to close the door, he spotted Brian across the way.

"It always rains on pitch 13 mate!" shouted Brian. "Never fails."

Geoff gave him the weakest of smiles and slammed the door shut.

"Dad, what's happened this time? All my photos are of you soaking wet," said Gail looking her father up and down.

"You've been taking photos all the time we've been here?" shuddered Geoff.

"Duh dad! That's what phones are for!" retorted Gail.

"Funny, I thought they were for making phone calls," muttered Geoff and headed into the bathroom.

Chapter 32

With Gail safely strapped in her seat and Mabel lying in her bed between him and Janice, Geoff waved goodbye to Brian and drove Woody along the pathway to the reception beside the exit. Along the route some of the campers stared at Woody, one or two taking the opportunity to gesticulate and point.

Janice covered her face with her hand and lowered her head. Geoff wished he could go faster than the five miles per hour limit on site. But he didn't want another violation to his name.

He parked up in the waiting bay, took a deep breath and opened the door.

"Please Geoff, no more disasters, I can't take any more." Janice said and gave him the stare he knew so well.

He jumped down from Woody and headed for reception. He actually felt himself clench his bottom cheeks as he entered in trepidation of facing Emperor Roger.

"Ah, Mr Watt, you're late," snorted Roger looking at his

Fitbit. "10.02am. Lucky you weren't three more minutes, there's a penalty for every five minutes if you're being escorted off the site."

Geoff rolled his eyes. "Ok, just tell me the damage," he said as Roger produced a huge push button calculator from a drawer behind the counter.

Roger tapped the buttons mumbling under his breath. Then tapped some more. He stopped and shook his head, letting out a whoosh of air from his pursed lips. Then he tapped some more, ending with a whistle you only get from a mechanic with bad news.

"£285.34" said Roger calmly, "and we're collecting for the Cumbrian Operatic Society this week if you'd like to round it up to a straight £300. Least you can do given the lead baritone's son is still in shock from his bike accident this morning."

"Whatever," sighed Geoff and pushed his card into the reader when Roger had given him the all clear.

Transaction completed, Roger then proceeded to read Geoff a prepared statement listing the offences he had been charged with and found guilty of and explained he could not enter the site again for 12 months commencing 10.15 hours today.

Roger was the judge, jury and executioner of Lakeside View Campsite and Geoff was a condemned man. He almost felt he should wait for Roger to place a black cloth on his head and send him to the gallows.

"If you can keep out of mischief at our other prime locations, and I will check Mr Watt, we will send you a questionnaire should you wish to book a stay again after your ban has been lifted. Section 23, subsection 4.6.5 states you cannot stay at any other of our sites in Cumbria until then. I bid you good day."

Geoff stood open mouthed desperately trying to think of something profound, witty or just plain sensible to say, but nothing was forthcoming.

"Errrr, thanks, it's been, well…different. First time and all that so we're just getting used to it," was all he could summon up.

He jumped back into Woody and turned on the engine.

"No problem love, all sorted," said Geoff and gave her his best loving husband smile.

"Yes, I'll wait for the credit card bill!" scowled Janice and off they went.

Chapter 33

The journey was mainly in silence, except for when Geoff heard a good tune on the radio and tried to get Janice to sing along. He tried his hardest when the inevitable Fleetwood Mac tune came on but this time Janice wasn't going to be Stevie Nicks to Geoff's Lindsay Buckingham. Geoff gave it up as a bad job.

"She'll be fine when she gets home and has a cup of tea," he thought and continued singing to himself.

As they travelled along the winding Cumbrian roads, Geoff and Janice took in the breathtaking scenery. Whatever had happened on their first trip away, nothing changed the beauty of their surroundings and that, in itself, was comforting to them both.

They passed several fellow motorhomers on the way and Geoff summoned up the energy to wave and smile to each one of them. Janice decided she'd abstain and leave him to it. She needed time to calm herself and remind herself of the qualities of the man next to her. The silence and concentrating on the landscape around her was slowly helping.

They had been on the motorway for a while when Geoff looked at the petrol gauge.

"I'll just stop to put some diesel in babe," said Geoff as he looked at the gauge on the dashboard. "Then we'll be all filled up when we head off again."

"Can't wait!" said Janice sarcastically and then felt a bit guilty when she saw Geoff's little face drop. "Yes ok love, next time will be much better," she said, feeling she should try a bit harder to accept Geoff was, well, just Geoff.

Geoff pulled Woody into the next petrol station and stopped at pump no 5 on the outside so he could make an easy exit *[you have to think of these things in a motorhome].*

As Geoff walked round to the pump, he looked up towards the entrance to the forecourt. At that moment, he saw the majestic sight of another motorhome pull in to refuel. But this wasn't just any motorhome. It was a *Gladiator 1000*. He stared open mouthed as it silently glided into position on the other side of the forecourt. His mouth remained open while the driver got out and proceeded to fill up.

Geoff couldn't take his eyes off it. He unscrewed the cap of the tank and picked up his pump. He glanced quickly making sure he'd chosen diesel, and shoved it into the opening where the cap had been.

He pressed the trigger and listened as the diesel began chugging through the hose and into the tank. He sniffed the smell and contemplated if he did like it or not. He wondered if everyone did that.

"I bet that takes forever to fill up," thought Geoff as he crooned over his ultimate motorhome desire. He traced every curve of the bodywork, every chrome fitting and the huge alloy wheels that wouldn't look out of place on a Ferrari. He remembered the luxurious interior, the hi-tec devices and the gold-trimmed bathroom. He was a world away now, absorbed in the moment.

As his mind scanned round the unit, he suddenly remembered how quickly the shower unit had filled up in the bathroom back at the motor show. He recalled the water, all that water, and his daring escape through the bedroom window. He felt a shiver down his spine and a strange wetness on his back and rapidly returned to the present day.

"This is taking ages," he thought as he glanced at the pump digital display. It had now clocked over £100 of fuel.

"What the heck…?!"

All of a sudden he heard a splashing sound and looked down to see diesel running down towards his feet. He turned off the pump and put it back in the holder.

Janice wound down the window. "What's the matter?" she said curiously but also slightly nervously.

"I think the diesel tank has got a leak," replied Geoff. "Must be at the top as it must be full by now. I'll have to ring the dealer as it's a bit dangerous to drive if it spills out on the road."

He went and explained to the attendant in the shop who told him he had to go off the forecourt to make a call on his mobile to avoid blowing up the petrol station.

"Could that really happen?" he thought as he exited the shop. "Surely loads of people use their mobile in petrol stations and I've never heard of one blowing up."

Anyway, given the last 48 hours, he wasn't going to

take that chance. He headed to the fence surrounding the forecourt, climbed over and called the dealer's number he had stored in his phone.

"West Yorkshire Motorhomes, where we turn your destination into a journey. Stuart speaking, how can I help you?"

Geoff knew it was the Stu they knew.

"Stu, hi it's Geoff, Geoff Watt."

"Oh, errr, hi Mr Watt. How are things?" replied Stu with an edge of shakiness in his voice.

"Well, I've just filled up with diesel after our first weekend away and I think the tank is leaking. It's spilled out when it got to the top."

"Erm, well it shouldn't do that Mr Watt. The only tank that overflows is the fresh water tank…Mr Watt,…Mr Watt?"

Geoff's face drained of colour as he lowered the mobile phone from his ear. He turned and looked at Woody and the liquid now slowly dripping from underneath the middle of the chassis. His brain tried to compute how he could possibly manage to mix up the petrol cap for the water cap. He heard an engine start and looked round to see the Gladiator 1000 glide off the forecourt and away to its next destination.

He slowly turned round to face Janice, still sat in the front seat of Woody. He saw her shrugging her shoulders and mouthing something like "What's the matter?" several times, each time a little more energetically. Geoff stood for a few seconds longer, a small amount of dribble now accumulated on his bottom lip and slowly started to run down his chin.

"Mr Watt, are you still there? Mr Watt?" came a distant voice an Geoff awkwardly returned the phone to his ear.

"Errrrm, I think we have a problem," he said gingerly. "I may have filled up the wrong tank."

"Tell me where you are and we'll get someone over," said Stu firmly. "Don't drive away whatever you do. You've got a petrol bomb on wheels!"

After telling Stu their location, Geoff walked slowly over to the petrol station attendant. Janice could see the man put his hand on his head and then shake his head slowly. Then he began pointing at Woody and then across to a space where people fill up with air and water.

"What's going on mum? Dad doesn't look very well and why is he walking like he's pooed himself?" said Gail peering out of her window.

"I dread to think love," replied Janice, "but I have a bad feeling about this."

Geoff returned to Woody and opened the door. He looked at Janice with the same look she had become accustomed to over their years together. Only this time he looked even more worried than usual.

"It seems I've put diesel in the water tank," confessed Geoff, his head drooping down like a naughty schoolboy in front of the headmaster.

"You've done what?!" exclaimed Janice. "How the hell? Of all the stupid things you've done, and there have been plenty, this is your finest hour man! What do we do now?"

"I spoke to Stu and they are sending someone over. I don't think we can drive Woody home love. It was the *Gladiator 1000*, I couldn't take my eyes of it and…"

"The what?" questioned Janice. "You mean that one

that was flooded at the show? You're not making any sense man."

"It was just there," said Geoff slowly, raising his finger to the empty pump where a couple of minutes ago stood the vehicle of his dreams.

Gail and Janice looked over to where he was pointing.

"He's completely lost it mum," said Gail. "Bethany's dad did the same thing after he lost their house in a poker game. He didn't know he was playing with people from the Mafia and tried to get out of it saying it was Beth's mums. When they started getting deliveries of pig's trotters in the post, he just lost it and had to be taken into some sort of rehab under a false name. The police got involved and had to rehouse them in Beddlesford and no one is allowed to know in case the Mafia find him."

Janice stared at Gail for a moment. "But you know Gail?" said Janice.

"Yes but I told Bethany I wouldn't tell anyone, swore on you and dad's life," replied Gail and did the sign of a cross over her chest.

"And now you've told us," continued Janice.

"Yes, but you won't tell anyone will you? Especially as they live in our street. Imagine if we got a pig's head delivered by Amazon!"

Janice shook her head trying to rid herself of the image of Geoff being pursued by the Mafia.

"It could be a better outcome than I'm planning for your dad!" she growled, looking at Geoff, who by now had almost melted into the ground.

Mabel had been lying on her bed listening to the whole conversation. She had heard the tone of voices rise and fall and witnessed the looks between mum and dad. Would this be a good time to ask to go out for a wee?

Geoff slowly moved Woody to the space suggested by the shop attendant. Janice and Gail sat on a low wall at the side of the forecourt while Geoff took Mabel for a short walk.

An hour, and three decidedly dodgy sandwiches from the petrol station later, and a car pulled onto the forecourt followed by a low loader truck.

Stu got out of the car and walked over to the Watts. Mabel recognised him instantly and began to bark. Stu stopped and felt his knees buckle slightly.

"Mabel, not now!" said Janice in the voice that told Mabel she meant business. She rearranged her mouth and withdrew her teeth bearing and obediently sat down next to her mum, looking like butter wouldn't melt.

Stu felt a little better and advanced forward.

"Bit of a pickle this" he said. "Lucky I was working the shift today and not Bob. He's been desperate to get called out for something like this. He's writing a book and always says the real life calamities are the best ones to write about – no one would ever believe it!"

"Ha ha, very funny," sulked Geoff. "Never mind about Bob and his book, what do we do now?" retorted Geoff, trying to divert attention from delving into the whys and wherefores of how the pickle had been made.

"Well, we will need to take you all back in my car and Tony here will follow with the vehicle on the low loader. We can take you home and then send someone round tomorrow to drain the tank and work out if it needs replacing. I hope not cos they're not cheap!"

Geoff glanced at Janice who was desperately trying to keep calm.

"Could have been worse love, at least we are all safe," offered Geoff.

"No thanks to you, you stupid man. We could all have been blown to kingdom come if you hadn't filled it to the top. And what if we'd wanted a drink on the way back. You'd have poisoned us if you hadn't succeeded in blowing us up!!"

Geoff decided he'd said enough and looked down at Mabel who had known better than to cause a fuss while the rest of the family had a meltdown.

"Look how many likes I've had!" shouted Gail as she presented her phone screen round the group like a trophy. "It's gone nuts! Thanks dad!"

"Errr, what's that for love?" enquired Geoff.

"I videoed you telling mum what happened and posted it to myembarassingdad.com. It's gone viral! Not even Destiny Smithson got that many when her dad recorded his own version of Time Warp on YouTube!"

Geoff sighed deeply. His dream weekend in his very own motorhome had not turned out how he had imagined. He looked to Janice for any crumbs of sympathy and was met with the same stare that had confronted him when he told her what he had done. At least it couldn't get any worse, he thought to himself.

"Let's get this baby on the truck Tony!" shouted Stu while he shepherded Geoff, Janice, Gail and Mabel towards his compact Ford Focus.

"The dog will need to go in the boot," he said as Mabel eyed him up and down. It's the hair you see, company policy doesn't allow dog hair on the seats." It wasn't true but Stu had no intention of driving with a crazy dog sat behind his head.

They all squeezed into the car while Tony manoeuvred Woody onto the truck.

Chapter 35

An hour later Stu pulled into Sycamore Avenue followed by Tony with Woody in tow. He parked up outside No. 6 and Tony stopped behind him covering the drive of No 8.

Before the Watts had all emerged from the car, Colin and Pat had appeared outside their front door.

"Hi there!" they shouted as they virtually ran down their drive and across the road. "Oh dear, what's been going on?"

By this time, other neighbours had heard the large truck and decided it must be worth a look.

"There's a technical problem," proclaimed Geoff. "Nothing you would understand Colin."

"Right Mr Watt," said Stu who had walked over with a clipboard and was busy writing down something important. "Tony will put the vehicle on the drive and drain the diesel from the water tank. Then we'll get someone over tomorrow to see if we can save it."

Geoff gave Stu a "why did you have to say that!" look and shook his head. By now a crowd had gathered around the entrance to No 6. Sheila Keane was at the front, wearing what can only be described as a 'going out dress'. At her side was Roger Keane, a rather rare event and made all the more awkward for Sheila as Mr Carson was standing next to him.

"So you put petrol in the water tank then Geoff?" Colin said, trying to hold back a smirk. There was a murmur in the crowd as the neighbours consulted each other, some nodding, others shaking their heads, one or two putting their hands over their mouths to hide their chuckles.

"Oooh Janice, that could have been very nasty," said Pat. "Did you have a nice time?"

Janice looked around at the faces of their neighbours, eager to absorb some new gossip on the street.

"We had a lovely time Pat. We got good weather, the site was very friendly and quiet, we met some nice people and we got time to relax and enjoy the outdoors. Everything we planned for."

Janice wondered how she'd managed to accompany her words with a convincing smile as she glanced around the crowd.

"Like Geoff said, just a technical problem at the petrol station. Could have happened to anyone." She grabbed Geoff's hand and squeezed it tightly. Whatever happened, she would be right by Geoff's side, through thick and thin.

"Yes babe," said Geoff as he scanned the group of neighbours as if looking for a dissenting voice or expression.

"We've had the time of our lives. Getting away from it all, getting back to nature, it's all good for the soul," he continued. "Some of you should try it, it'll give you something worthwhile to do!"

The faces in the crowd turned to shock and perhaps there was a hint of guilt on one or two of them as it dawned on them they were grouped together like a flock of vultures, waiting for the pickings after a kill.

Just at that moment, a police car approached and parked up in front of No 4. An officer got out and walked over to the gathering. The neighbours who had begun to walk away turned round and decided the show may not yet be over.

Mabel began to growl, sensing this man in a uniform was not looking very friendly. Janice bent down and whispered something in her ear which seemed to calm her a little.

"Anyone here called Mr Watt?" said the policeman.

The group all turned their attention from the officer to Geoff, leaving no doubt who went by that name.

"Errr, yes that's me," said Geoff nervously. "What can I do for you officer?"

"We'd like you to come down to the station sir. We need to talk to you about some damage caused to a luxury motorhome at the recent show."

"Oh," said Geoff nervously. "Why do you want to talk to me?"

"When we were cleaning up the damage in the bathroom, we found a ticket to the show stuck to the toilet bowl. It was pre-ordered so luckily it had the name on it. Didn't take too long to find out who had ordered it once we'd got over all that GDPR nonsense."

Geoff looked at Janice who had loosened her grip on his hand. He then looked at Gail who was feverishly tapping into her phone screen. Then down to Mabel who licked his hand as if trying to give him her support. His eyes scanned the rest of faces – Stu, Tony, Sheila, Colin, Pat and the rest of the street, all staring at him in disbelief. This news was gold dust. You could almost hear the cogs whirring as they thought about how they were going to share this latest exclusive.

"If you'd like to step into the vehicle sir. We'll just take you down to the station so you can help us with our enquiries."

"It's ok love, I can sort it," said Geoff turning to Janice. "I'll be back for tea."

And with that he followed the policeman into the car.

Janice stood open mouthed as she watched her husband disappear into the back seat. She turned to see Tony jump into Woody and start the engine and then to Stu who was scribbling something on his clipboard. Her gaze panned round the crowd again at the faces waiting in expectation for a comment from the stricken wife.

"It's a case of mistaken identity," she declared. "He'll be back for tea. Nothing more to see here. Come on Gail, let's get inside a put the kettle on. I need a cuppa. Come on Mabel."

"I'm sure that's right," said Pat reassuringly. "If there's anything we can do…"

Janice didn't wait to reply. The next sound was the front door of No. 6 slamming. The Watt's Show was over and the crowd slowly dispersed chattering and gesticulating as they went. Stu guided Tony and Woody into the drive and Tony set to work draining the tank.

Gail ran upstairs to her bedroom, already on a video

call with one of her followers. Janice looked out of the window and sighed. She thought about her husband and the misadventures they had experienced this weekend. She thought about her sketching in the beautiful spot in the woods and a smile began to draw across her lips.

"I'll finish that sketch off in watercolours," she thought. "It will be a lovely reminder of our first trip away in Woody."

"Come on Mabel, I think you need a drink."

In the back of the police car, Geoff's mind was in overdrive. He cast his mind back to the day he went online and purchased the tickets for the motorhome show. The tickets that had lead to him buying Woody, who had taken them on their first adventure into the world of motorhome living. The tickets that had brought them the opportunity to change the way they lived. The tickets that had resulted in him sitting in the back of a police car.

Did he regret it? Any of it? Not a chance.

"Life is for living," he thought to himself. "And this is only the beginning…"

Acknowledgements

Debbie Akal (aka 'Debs'):
For my wife's continued support in pursuing my ambitions and providing (perhaps) the odd idea for content!

Abbey Akal (aka 'Tink'):
For my youngest daughter who has provided me with soulful inspiration and support whether she realises it or not.

Dave Bull (davebull.co.uk):
For his creativity and expertise in capturing what was in my head onto such brilliant cover artwork.

All Motorhomers and Campervanners (aka 'Sliders'):
For your love of travel and exploring all nature has to offer. Keep providing those wonderful moments for me to take inspiration from.